THE
ROAD
GHOST

D. B. Drumm

A DELL BOOK

Published by
Dell Publishing Co., Inc.
1 Dag Hammarskjold Plaza
New York, New York 10017

Dell ® TM 681510, Dell Publishing Co., Inc.

ISBN: 0-440-17469-4

Printed in the United States of America
First printing—October 1985

DD

SUICIDE RUN

The bullets had hit her in the stomach, making wounds no larger than dimes. Traveler could have put his fist through the exit wounds in her back, though.

Something within him snapped. He reached over to the rack and removed his HK91. He took two extra clips and stuck them in his belt. He got out of the car, rifle in hand.

"Kiel," Hill whispered, "are you nuts?"

Traveler stood at the top of the sand dune. Seventy or eighty armed monks gathered at the foot.

"You have killed the woman," Traveler yelled.

The monks cheered, waving their rifles and burning spears.

"Now," Traveler said softly, "you'll pay for it."

The Traveler Saga

FIRST, YOU FIGHT
KINGDOM COME
THE STALKERS
TO KILL A SHADOW
ROAD WAR
BORDER WAR

1

He was a dead man.

The gaunt figure astride the malformed horse swatted a gnat away from his cheek. The slap stung like hell. He rubbed the red spot growing on his stubble.

Well, almost a dead man. He squinted into the harsh white light of the desert sun. The large jagged wound on his forehead throbbed incessantly. No matter that the wound had healed into a crimson scar. He still felt the blood. He still heard the explosion deadening his senses.

The horse stumbled. The rider tried to pull in the reins. But the horse collapsed on its right side, uttering a resigned sigh as it fell.

The rider, his reflexes still drowsily intact despite his exhaustion, kicked himself free of the beast and tumbled onto the hot sand. His face smacked into the grit. And he swallowed a mouthful of the stuff. He got to his knees and spat out as much as he could.

No use. The sand stuck to his tongue. He burst into a coughing fit. He felt like he was wearing a plastic bag over his face. He couldn't breathe. The heat. The sand. The dehydration. He almost felt like laughing. So this was how it ended.

The mighty Traveler. The postnuclear survivor to end all survivors. Hero to some. Devil to many. He had come a long way to wind up dying in the middle of the sun-baked nowhere.

It had started so long ago.

He had been a military "advisor" in the sleepy Latin American country of El Hiagura. He had just survived a dose of an experimental neurotoxin that was supposed to drive its victims mad when inhaled, a chemical designed to heighten a man's senses to the point of excruciating pain. He was on his way back to the States to begin a life-saving treatment when the bombs fell.

World War III . . . the nuclear nightmare that people had feared for four decades.

For sixteen years he had survived in the wasteland that used to be America. The effects of the neurotoxin had left him with a sixth sense. It wasn't anything supernatural, but it often struck others as such. He could have been a king had he remained in America once the new government formed in the year 2006. Instead he chose to leave. Opt for a happy ending.

A dry giggle rattled in his throat. He stared at the mutant horse in front of him. The creature's eyes were caked with pus and fluid. Its nostrils were cracked and inflamed. Its tongue was white, sliding over lips caked with dried white froth. A tumor in the middle of its head gave the creature a football-shaped profile. The Elephant Horse.

Traveler patted the creature on its bloated forehead.

So much for happy endings.

The creature wheezed as it struggled to breathe. Its swollen stomach heaved and shuddered. Traveler felt genuine affection for the beast. They had met on the road, two loners, lost and confused. Joining forces, they headed north, toward distant mountains. It didn't look like either one would make it to those mountains now.

The water had run out this morning; the food, the morning before.

The horse pressed its nuzzle into Traveler's outstretched hand. Traveler would have shot the creature and put it out of its misery had he a gun. But he had lost all his modern weaponry in the accident. He shuddered, trying to shut out the images of the blast and the fire, the screaming, the clawing, as the boat went down. As far as he knew, he was the only survivor.

He smirked to himself. Survivor indeed.

Traveler stared at the pitiable creature before him. He still had a knife on him: a Fairbairn-Sykes fighting knife. It was small and straight-bladed. It weighed less than a half pound, was twelve inches in length and razor sharp. With a quick slash he could have slit the beast's throat.

The mutant horse whinnied softly. Before the war, before the genetically damaged herds bred and spawned countless deformities across the land, this horse might have been something proud and beautiful.

Traveler left the knife in its sheath. He ran a calloused finger across the deep slash down his forehead.

Traveler slid closer to the horse. He lifted its head and placed it on his lap. He stroked the animal's matted mane, listening to its labored breathing. The breathing became rasping. The rasping turned to croaking.

Finally, under the relentless stare of the sun, the horse shivered. Its legs flailed in one last seizure. It stopped breathing.

Traveler pulled himself from beneath the creature's bloated head and stood before the fallen animal. He felt guilty about leaving it there, yet he knew it would be sixty times more stupid to try to bury the thing.

He shook his head in amazement. That explosion must have done more damage to his head than he had thought. In his mercenary days, he must have left thousands of human beings, both good and god-awful, on the roadside—dead and dying. He never thought twice about it either.

Now here he was, feeling sorry for a fucking ugly piece of horseflesh.

He turned his back on the carcass and faced the mountains that loomed ahead. Once upon a time he had called himself Traveler because that was what he did best. It was time to live up to his name once again. He took four steps forward and passed out from both the heat and the exhaustion.

In his mind he saw faces. He was on a boat—a yacht. Sailing into the sunset just like a movie hero, with his girl at his side. Jan. A light-skinned Indian with eyes that could melt the hardest of hearts. Link was there too. A towering black man. An ally. A friend. With Link was Rosalita. They hadn't been at sea for more than two weeks when a shadow covered the vessel and an explosion tore apart what Traveler hoped would be an endless string of violence-free tomorrows.

Traveler slowly opened his eyes.

A shadow blotted out the sun.

He gritted his teeth and waited for the blast to tear his life apart a second time.

No blast came. The shadow above him emitted a blood-curdling shriek. Traveler focused his sun-blasted eyes and saw that the thing above him was a vulture. He slowly shifted his eyes to his left. Two other birds of prey were busily tearing into the flesh of the horse.

Clearly the bird towering above Traveler's face wasn't into horsemeat.

Traveler slowly eased his hand toward his belt. Suddenly the bird reared its head back for a quick stab at Traveler's unblinking eyes. Before it could plunge its beak downward, the knife blade had slashed across its neck, neatly severing its head.

Traveler's movement was so quick, so violent, that the bird didn't even have a chance to cry out. Traveler grabbed the staggering creature. Meat would have to wait. Fighting off nausea, he plunged his lips into the blood spurting from the knife wound and sucked deep.

Traveler closed his eyes and thought of anything else as he took the nourishing substance into his system. He opened his eyes after a minute or two. The two other vultures were still at the horse. Neither one paid any mind to Traveler. They didn't seem to mind sharing the dining area with another species.

Traveler shuddered. He clutched his stomach. His entire body reeked of blood and phlegm. He wasn't a big man, five foot nine or so, right now he couldn't have weighed more than one fifty. His slim body doubled up in a spasm as his digestive tract battled with its newfound nourishment.

Traveler grimaced.

Gradually the spasms subsided. He felt his strength returning. He got to his feet and took a deep breath of stagnant afternoon air.

Then he sensed it. Something was wrong. He glanced around. The vultures at the horse were gone. Traveler squinted into the distance. The desert seemed empty, yet every fiber in his body told him that something was closing in on him, and fast.

It was then that he spotted it.

A solid wall of darkness rumbling toward him from the south. Traveler stood in the open, totally vulnerable. There were no rocks to hide behind. No trees. No wrecked autos. Nothing.

He trotted over to the remains of the horse and knelt, face down, beside it.

The air seemed to thunder. The sky seemed to threaten to explode. His skin was raked by tiny pellets of grit that stung like bullets.

The shadow wall blotted out the sun.

Traveler huddled next to the foul-smelling carcass.

The dust storm tore him from his spot and sent him tumbling out into the desert, out into unconsciousness, out into the unknown.

2

He couldn't see the sun.

He couldn't see the mountains.

He couldn't even see the desert anymore. For a moment Traveler toyed with the idea that he might be blind. But, no, he was sprawled, belly down, on the desert floor, the massive storm now roaring in front of him, heading away from the sand dunes and toward the approaching twilight.

Traveler knew that he wouldn't last long in the cold desert night. The thought made him angry. It was a real piss to die like this with so many questions left unanswered. What had happened to his friends on the boat: Jan, Link, Rosalita? Traveler blinked away a single tear. What had happened to the damned boat?

Nothing made sense. He had set sail following the rebirth of America. Traveler, Link, and two of Traveler's old military pals from El Hiagura, Orwell and Hill, had finally beaten down the marauding army run by the last President of the deranged America of the 1990s, Andrew Frayling.

A roadrat turned patriot named John Marchmont Jefferson seemed like a sure thing to reunify the fragmented country. The first postnuke President. All seemed tranquil. So Traveler had decided to split.

What had happened to the new United States?

So many questions would be left unanswered. Damn it.

Traveler sighed and waited for the freezing desert night to

slowly numb his senses. The dust began to clear. He found himself staring into an inky, star-filled sky.

The desert was silent. The stars were bright. A full moon shone down. Perhaps this was a good time to die, after all. Better to die at the hands of nature than at the blade of a cannibal mutant or a marauding roadrat.

The stars before Traveler began to twinkle, then disappear. Traveler tried to pull himself up into sitting position. A silhouette was blacking out the stars. Someone, or something, was coming. He was too weak to sense exactly what it was shambling toward him but, from a distance the shadowshape looked a little like a dinosaur. It seemed to have a human torso but its bottom appeared to have four large legs. It carried a spear. It wore a horned helmet. A large, feathered shield hung from its side.

Traveler shook his head in amazement.

It was a man dressed in haphazardly constructed ceremonial garb riding a buffalo.

"Hoi, hoi, hoi," the warrior astride the buffalo croaked. "It's the travelin' boy. Just stay where you are. I came down from the stars. I'm gonna try to help you so don't cringe at my scars."

The man astride the buffalo slid off its back. He was dressed like an old-fashioned Indian, the kind that Hollywood once had Italians play. His skin, however, was one massive wad of scar tissue. It was thick and gray, almost lizardlike. The man's face was pulled back tight, ashen-colored. He had skull-like eyes, a nonexistent nose, and a mouth twisted into a permanent pout. He looked like a fish.

Traveler gazed at the man. "Blast victim?" he rasped.

"Nope," the man said, bending over Traveler with a canteen. "Third degree. Ooooowheee. My house was on fire and it spread to me. I was eight at the time, nearly blew my mind, but before I could heal, the nurses all squealed, the city blew apart, and the world was unreal. So I fit right in, you dig it, Jim? In a tidal wave of mutants I was right in the swim."

Traveler raised the canteen to his lips. He had to fight the impulse to gulp the contents down. If he did that, he'd be in big trouble. He let a few drops touch his lips. The water stung. He wet his swollen tongue, then allowed a trickle to run down his throat.

"Do you always talk like that?" he asked the man.

"Naaah," the man said, leaning up against the buffalo. "Sometimes I talk black jive. Sometimes I act like an Indian. I do a pretty fair Mexican too. I figure that, since I have no skin to speak of, no race, I represent all skins, all races. I can do what I want. I can be any minority that I want to be, mon ami."

"What's your name?"

"Rat Du Bois. It means 'rat of the woods.' "

"How did you know I was out here?"

"Well, me and Bill here," he said, pointing toward the bison, "Love our peyote. It's been seventeen years since the big bang, boyo. Seventeen years of peyote. Does something to your senses, you know? You feel things. Amazing stuff. Sometimes you'd swear you can hear flowers and animals thinking. I almost had an out-of-body experience once. I got stuck in neutral though. I did manage to roll out of my sleeping bag. The zipper actually talked to me."

He shrugged philosophically. "Anyhow, I just *felt* you out here. I can pick up disturbances pretty well. Troubled spirits and all that. And, man, if you don't mind me saying so, your spirit is an encyclopedia of troubles."

He tossed a small package at Traveler. "Here, eat this."

Traveler unwrapped the package. "A Snickers bar?"

"You find the damndest things when you travel around enough, but you should know that, right? They call you Traveler, right?"

"Some did."

"They still do. People describe you to a 'T' up north. The combat fatigues, the boots, the bandanna, the black T-shirt. They've memorized you, man. You're the king of the road, Traveler."

"I used to be."

"Yeah, I heard you retired. What brings you out hereabouts?"

"I'll be damned if I know. Where am I, anyhow?"

"Welcome, my man, to the land of sand. If you'd like to know, you're in Mexico. There's fanatics on your left and rebels on your right and a madman right before you in the full moonlight."

"Please, cut the poetics!"

Du Bois sighed and climbed back on the buffalo. "Sorry. I get bored sometimes. I tend to stay away from other people. They take one look at me and freak out. They usually assume I'm some sort of deranged mutant or a genetic experiment. By the time I explain to them that it's third-degree burns, they're either running from me or shooting at me.''

Traveler munched the Snickers bar. "I didn't mean to snap, it's just that I have no idea what the fuck is going on. Anywhere. With anybody.''

Du Bois nodded sagely. "Well, you came to the right place to be confused. This area is turning into a nightmare, man. Me and Bill are packing it in and heading north of the border. President Jefferson— the new guy?—he's getting things pretty well organized. You can actually ride along the roads of California without getting eaten these days.''

"Impressive.''

"If I were you, I'd get my act together and hit the road again. This place is getting really looney tunes. Bad vibes.''

Traveler got to his feet. "How far is it to the States?''

"Maybe two hundred miles, give or take a mountain.''

Du Bois stopped suddenly. Traveler gazed into the man's fishlike face. It shone in the moonlight, a portrait of mystery. A small chuckle emerged the man's lips. "But you have a lot to do before you skiddoo. There's fighting to be done, battles to be won, babies meant to cry, and icons meant to die.''

"You're crazy,'' Traveler said.

"I know.'' Du Bois giggled. He pointed to a particularly large sand dune to his left. "On the other side of that pile of shit is a small town. It's called . . . Do you know what the Spanish is for 'Town of Dead Dreams'?''

"No.''

"Me neither. I should learn, though. The place is a real burg. Used to still be a honkie hangout. Life-styles of the rich and infamous. Roadrats trashed it years ago. Nothing left standing but the lawn jockeys. The roadrats looted only the big stuff, though. Very materialistic. There are still some supplies there. Couple of junker cars. You can probably get one of them running if you tinker with it enough. Just don't take too long. This whole area will be overrun soon.''

Du Bois nudged the buffalo. The animal turned around and walked slowly back into the night.

"Overrun with who?'' Traveler called.

"Bad mamajammas, daddy-o. Keep your eyes open. You have a lot to accomplish in a very short period of time.''

"I don't understand."

"You don't have to, bro, you're just a small piece in a very big, very cosmic puzzle. Hoi, hoi, hoi. Watch your ass, travelin' boy."

Traveler watched the vision slowly disappear into the swirling sand. He strained his ears to hear what the man was muttering as he rode off. Du Bois wasn't talking, however. He was singing.

"Sha-boom. Sha-boom. Yada-da-da-da-da-da-da-da-da-da."

Traveler shrugged his shoulders and headed toward the large mountain of grit.

It was time to enter the nightmare in earnest.

3

Walking into what was left of the settlement, Traveler knew what Du Bois had meant about a city of dead dreams. The place looked like a consumer's guide to hell. The houses must have been very expensive once—sprawling edifices with large grounds and swimming pools. Now swirling driveways extended into nowhere. Overgrown foliage mingled with the skeletal remains of whoever had been unlucky enough to get caught unawares when the roadrats rode in.

The place smelled stale. Even the dirt seemed bad.

Traveler walked into a small shed in the back of one of the ransacked homes. It was probably the servants' quarters. He found some canned goods and made a quick breakfast of some refried beans and Spanish rice.

He then set about the task of survival.

After ransacking several garages and toolsheds, he found what he needed to fashion a few basic weapons. Discovering a cache of .45-caliber ammunition, he decided to make a handgun. He gathered a steel pipe, some couplings, wood, tape, elastic bands, and assorted bric-a-brac and, settling down in a long-abandoned shed next to a brown and black garden, began the process.

Using a bullet as a gauge, he drilled a hole in the pipe and fitted it into the coupling. Then, using nails, a pipe plug, and a metal strap, he fashioned a crude barrel and firing mechanism. He sawed thick wood into a stock. When he placed the pipe into a hole cut into the wood, Traveler had the basics of a handgun. By attaching a small rubber strap to the firing pin, he could "cock" the gun and then fire it. The only problem was that the gun was good for only one real shot. After that, it would have to have its barrel cleaned out with a metal rod before being reloaded, like an old-fashioned breech-loading musket. Still, it was better than using a spear.

For two days Traveler labored. He constructed nail grenades. Molotov cocktails. Mortar scrap mines. Every bit of metal, gasoline, gunpowder, and rubbish he could find was a possible weapon. Using a mixture of nitric acid and urine, he prepared a batch of highly explosive (and unpredictable) urea nitrate.

For some reason as yet unknown to him, he was preparing to make a last stand in this town. Trouble was coming. He knew that. He understood that.

He just didn't know where it was coming from or why.

As he continued his work, his mood gradually improved. He was a man who was used to being alone. Some people found the prospect unnerving. Traveler found it comforting. He never talked to himself. Never muttered. Never whistled. Never sang. He merely focused his attention on the work at hand and got down to it.

For all he knew, all the loved ones he had recently acquired were dead. For the second time in his life, he found himself beginning anew. Alone. This time around he wasn't angry about it. He was resigned to the fact that some people were destined never to be settled. Maybe he was one. Maybe he could be at peace only when he was on the run.

On the third day Traveler managed to get an old VW Bug running. The thing dated back to the 1970s. That made it nearly forty years old. He just might make it to the border in the contraption. It got good mileage. That he knew. On the negative side, however, the little car would run on unleaded gasoline only. His customized Meat Wagon, one of the last Wankel engine jobs made before the war, would run on *anything* burned from traditional fuel to good booze, even nail polish remover.

He toiled endlessly on the little blue Beetle. He couldn't complain. It beat the hell out of galloping across the desert on a mutated horse.

He set up headquarters in what was left of an old restaurant: Chez Fantasy. He fashioned a bunk behind the bar. In case anyone rode into town without him realizing it, the bar provided good cover. He hid the VW in the back, under a mound of collapsed trellis work. All that kept him from leaving now were a few modifications in the car.

There was no way he could adequately bulletproof the thing. Metal sheeting would serve as solid armor but it would weigh the car down too much. All he could do was plug the side and back windows with straightened fenders from other cars, line the inside of the Bug with a thin layer of house siding, and keep his fingers crossed.

He planned to remove the backseat and fill a child's small vinyl swimming pool with gasoline. It would serve as a fuel bladder, an extra tank just in case Du Bois had misjudged the distance between this town and the border. Traveler didn't want to think about what would happen if the gasoline bladder was hit during a firefight. So he didn't.

Nearly a week after staggering into the former resort town, Traveler was ready to roll. He slept during the final day and prepared to leave in the early evening, when twilight made motoring across the desert feasible.

As he stuffed the last of his rations into the car, he became aware of an ever-increasing presence of danger. Grabbing his slapdash pistol and a few nail grenades, he ran back into the restaurant and took his place behind the bar. He had rigged the place with several strategically placed booby traps but he would really hate to use them. If he found himself going one on one with more than a dozen well-armed men right about now, all the inventive booby traps in the world wouldn't prevent him from becoming dead meat.

Traveler heard the roar of a truck outside in the streets. Hoofbeats were reverberating down the block as well. Traveler slowly stuck his head over the bar. His hair was close-cropped, almost punkish, and he wore a black bandanna to keep it in place. In the deepening twilight, he blended in well with the burned and twisted mahogany background.

Outside a troop transport pulled up next to what used to be a curb. Traveler held his breath, expecting some sort of paramilitary expedition to pile out. He kept his surprise in check as a group of monks leapt out, carrying light assault rifles. Traveler swallowed hard. They were Armalite AR-180s. He knew all about them. He used to carry one himself. They were good at nailing a human up to 150 yards, but they were pretty damned effective up to 450 if need be.

Several black-robed monks on horses galloped up to the truck, followed by an obese man on a white stallion. Traveler didn't know whether to laugh or to cry. The mountainous fellow was dressed up in a bishop's outfit. Either that or he was trying to pass himself off as the bargain-basement version of the pope.

"Where is she?" the man in the red and gold robes inquired.

"There's no sign of her, your Holiness," one of his black-cowled minions replied.

The leader pointed a large staff in the direction of the restaurant. "Have you checked in there?"

"No, your Holiness, we were just about to."

Traveler sank behind the bar. Just his luck. He was about to blow himself up into kingdom come while being attacked by a group of marauding monks. If there was a God, he had a pretty off-the-wall sense of humor.

He heard the door to the bar open. Footsteps. Two, maybe three, monks were walking toward him. In about three seconds one of them would step on a nail mine. That would bring more monks. More gunfire. More shit than Traveler could handle.

The sound of automatic fire and shouts from outside caused the monks to turn and leave the building. Traveler poked his head up from behind the bar as the three men rejoined their robed leader. The religious army was holding back, not returning the fire. Someone was heading up the street toward them. Traveler couldn't see that far out of the restaurant. What next—Ninja nuns?

Several jeeps roared onto the scene. Out of the vehicles leapt several weatherbeaten men in dark blue. They were heavily armed. Bearded. Around their ankles they wore tattered American flags. It was a half-assed insignia Traveler had thought he had seen the last of: Old Glory. Glory Boys . . . the twisted remnants of the United States Army.

But President Frayling was dead. The Glory Boys' key base

was obliterated. Traveler had made sure of that. So who the hell were these goons?

A man wearing a captain's insignia addressed the robed maniac. "Sorry, your Holiness, but this area is off-limits."

"Ah, Captain Memphis, I will excuse your insolence this time but, as you know, temporal matters do not deter us when it comes to affairs of faith."

The captain rolled his eyes. "Your Holiness, my men and I do appreciate all the aid you've given us in the past few months, but this is a military area, you could very easily be killed."

The robed man raised his hoglike visage heavenward. "Our Lord will save us, son. The avenging God of the Nouveau Testament will allow us to succeed in our holy war."

"But—"

The man was not deterred. "I, Gordon I, Pope of the Plains, Leader of the Right to a Good Life Church, have been sent on this Earth to prevent catastrophe; to catch this woman, Maria, before she can sprout her seed upon this Earth. Before she can plunge us all into a new and dangerous era!"

"That's all very well and good, your Excellency, but—"

"And no one, Captain, no one or no thing will deter me in my task."

The captain heaved his shoulders and sighed. "Did you find her?"

"No. But she is nearby. We *know* it."

"Then may I suggest you leave now? We're on a patrol here, your Holiness, searching out dangerous rebels. I would hate to have you caught in the crossfire."

The pope twisted his puffy face into a semblance of a smile. He nodded silently at his monks. The cowled men with the guns jumped back in the troop transport. The pope spurred his stallion into a gallop. The mounted monks trotted off after him, followed by the sputtering truck.

Captain Memphis climbed back into his jeep. He motioned his men to follow him. Within seconds the streets were clear again. Traveler cautiously left the shelter afforded him by the bar and stepped outside into the gathering dusk.

A roar broke into the silence of the night.

Something was heading down the middle of the town, fast.

Traveler didn't have time to run back into the restaurant.

The vehicle was heading right for him. It was black, battered, and armored like a tank.

Traveler couldn't believe his eyes.

It was the Meat Wagon.

4

Traveler stood, transfixed, as the Meat Wagon rumbled to a halt. Years ago he had stolen the teardrop-shaped vehicle and customized it into the ultimate survival vehicle. Iron shutters were installed across every window to protect the interior from stray shots. The inside of the small van was lined with bulletproof vests. Chain-mail skirts protected the tires. It was equipped with rooftop machine-gun turrets, a Geiger counter, and a comprehensive weapons rack.

He didn't know whether to run up to the vehicle or run away from it. Depending on who was behind the wheel, Traveler was about to have his ass either saved or obliterated.

The driver's door swung open and a short, bulky man in army fatigues emerged. He stood next to the car and snorted at Traveler. A second figure emerged from the passenger's side: a tall, imposing black man, his face heavily scarred. He, too, regarded Traveler with a bemused look.

"I told you he was down here," the short man said.

"Yeah. When this guy sends out bad vibes, you can feel them a thousand miles away."

The small, sandy-haired man grinned at Traveler. "How's it goin', fearless leader?"

Traveler walked up to Hill and Orwell and embraced them. "It's goin' better now," he said to the driver. "A lot better."

Hill nodded toward Orwell. "Nothing seems to be able to break up the team, huh?"

Orwell allowed himself a chuckle before letting his face drop into a scowl. "This place is *intense*."

Grabbing a heavy assault rifle from the car, he moved cautiously down the street. Traveler reached into the Wagon and pulled out a 12-gauge riot shotgun. Hill and Orwell had kept the van well stocked.

Within seconds the trio lapsed back into a natural combat-ready stance; a routine they had honed down to a science years before as "military advisors" in El Hiagura.

"Where can we stash the van?" Hill asked. "The Glory Boys have been on our ass all day."

Traveler pointed to the restaurant. "Pull it around back. I have a VW buried back there. There's enough cover for two cars."

Hill climbed into the Wagon and maneuvered it behind the building, leaving Traveler and Orwell in front. "How the hell did you get down here?" Orwell asked.

"I only wish I knew," Traveler replied. "What are you guys doing here? What happened to Jefferson? Who are these Glory Boys?"

Orwell had to smile. "You want those answers in order?"

"Sorry," Traveler replied, rubbing the scar on his forehead. "I feel like I've been away a long time."

"You have." Orwell nodded. "Close to a year."

Traveler tried to hide his surprise. He'd been wandering longer than he had thought. The boat. The explosion. It had seemed like only yesterday.

Orwell slumped into a squatting position. "After you split, Hill and I hung out with Jefferson. He's a good man. He's trying his best to begin the United States again. It's slow going, though. He's moving from territory to territory. I think the fact that he's an ex-roadrat helps a lot. Most of the roadscum respect him. A lot of the bandits and bikers are falling into line. All along we figured there would be some resistance to a new unification movement but not much. We were wrong."

"Glory Boys?"

"You got it. When we wiped out the Glory Boys up north we never figured there'd be a whole mess of them south of the border. Before he bought the farm, Frayling sent them down here to 'recruit' new members."

"Slaves."

"Uh-huh. When our Glory muchachos found out about Frayling's death, they doubled their recruiting efforts. They're planning to invade the States and kill Jefferson. Their leader is some bozo named Scar. We're not sure who he is or where he comes from."

Traveler turned as Hill emerged from the restaurant. "Nice setup in there," Hill acknowledged. "You serve quiche?"

"Fuck you."

Orwell grinned. "Anyhow, these Glory Boys have been creeping up the coast toward California. They've mined most of the areas near the coastline. They've been blowing boats out of the water in the Pacific like crazy. They've gotten hold of a couple of Mexican planes, World War II Air Force surplus, and have been bombing the shit out of any ship they see."

Traveler grimaced. That explained the shadow he saw before the explosion destroyed his own boat. "Yeah," he muttered. "I know all about it."

Hill and Orwell exchanged glances. They didn't ask Traveler about the rest of his shipmates. They didn't want to know.

Hill picked up the thread. "We both figured you were in trouble down here. We sensed it, you know?"

Traveler nodded. The neurotoxin they all took in had both expanded their sensory skills and created sort of a telekinetic bond between them. He *did* know what Hill was talking about.

"So," Orwell continued, "we decided to take a little pleasure trip. Unfortunately, we ran into the reconstituted Glory Boys on the way. We had underestimated their strength."

"By a *lot*," Hill said, shaking his head in disbelief. "These guys are fucking crazy, man. Half of them are drunks, the other half are doped up on some weird hallucinogenic shit. They're like those old Japanese kamikaze guys during World War Two. They don't care if they live or die. They just charge you, man."

"We figured that as soon as we found you," Orwell said, "we'd make a beeline for the border and clue Jefferson in on what's going on."

Hill finished the thought. "If we don't slap these suckers down right now and fast, the new United States isn't going to be very united for very long."

Traveler stared at the full moon above him. "I saw some

troops this afternoon," he said. "They weren't Glory Boys. They looked like priests or monks."

"The Good Lifers." Hill grunted. "More insanity."

"That I figured out for myself," Traveler said. "But who the hell are they?"

"Kooks, mostly," Hill said, "but *armed* kooks. They're new to us too. But, from what we can figure, they're a paramilitary group that uses a religion as a front for a power base. Right now they run the southern half of Mexico and they're pretty well into South America."

Orwell explained, "South America has always been a Christian continent. After the war a few enterprising powermongers fled down here, sized up the situation, and preyed on the superstitions of the folks to start up a whole new army.

"The Good Life Church has embarked on a wave of missionary work that makes the Nazi movement look casual. They're real Bible thumpers. . . ."

"Yeah," Hill added. "Except that their Bible was 'discovered' about ten years ago by a man named Gordon."

"I saw him. The pope. He mentioned a Nouveau Testament."

"Right," Hill said. "We figure he wrote it to fit his needs. The guy's an ex-merc. He used to fight for whoever had the biggest check in hand. A real saint. His god has appointed him to unify South America, start a massive government—"

"And take over the world," Traveler finished.

"How did you guess?" Orwell smirked.

"He didn't seem too sure of himself this afternoon," Traveler said.

"Yeah, well." Hill grinned. "Here's the fun part. About nine months ago old Gordy runs across a *real* missionary. An old bearded geezer named Ruez, Father Emmanuel Ruez. Now, I don't know if Ruez was playing with a full deck at the time, but he seemed like a *real* holy man. No gold. No guns. Just an open house and plenty of food for his flock, right?

"Of course, he doesn't give in to Gordy's demands to join the Good Life group. So old Gordo decides to off him. Big slaughter. Makes My Lai look like Sunday brunch. Before he goes, though, Ruez tells Gordo that a new messiah will be born on Earth, a messiah that will be fathered by one of Gordo's own monks. This ecclesiastical Nazi will wipe out all false religions and restore Christianity back to the world. Not only that, but he will help the human race make contact with their outer space brethren.''

Traveler grunted. ''Sounds pretty twisted.''

Orwell stretched, placing his rifle on the ground at his side. ''Yeah. But Gordo's taking no chances. He's had all his main monks castrated . . . just in case. Unfortunately, one servant girl managed to get knocked up before his Holiness cornered the market on wang-dang-doodles.''

''Her name Maria?'' Traveler asked.

''That's a bingo,'' Hill said. ''Gordy-boy's convinced that Maria's kid is the new messiah. He's been on her case ever since.''

Traveler walked back into the restaurant. ''I'm sure glad the world is getting back to normal.''

''Me too,'' Hill said, ''so what I suggest is, after we get a few hours sleep, let's get the fuck out of here. The longer we stay, the greater the odds of our staying forever, if you catch my drift.''

Orwell followed Traveler into the restaurant. ''We have enough rations in the Wagon for three,'' he said. ''We should be able to make it no sweat if we leave soon. The Glory Boys are massing toward the border. If we wait too long, we'll never make it alive.''

Traveler stretched out on the floor. ''No problem. I have no desire to stay here any longer than I have to.''

Hill entered the room and placed his rifle on the floor. ''I have to hand it to you, Kiel,'' he said to the man who now called himself Traveler. ''I mean, we would have found you just on gut instinct, but it was pretty clever of you to set off that homing beacon.''

Traveler sat up. ''Homing beacon?''

''Yeah,'' Hill said, curling up into fetal position. ''We've been following it for two days.''

Traveler leapt to his feet. ''I never set off any homing signal.''

Orwell got to his feet and grabbed his rifle in one feline move. ''Shit.'' He glanced at a device on his wrist. It looked like a watch but was composed of small, pulsating dots of light. ''He's right. The beacon is still putting out but it's not coming from in here.''

The black man ran into the street, rifle held firmly in his left hand, his right wrist extended in front of his body. Hill followed. Traveler, grabbing a flashight, brought up the rear.

"It's coming from in here," Orwell said, pointing to an abandoned drugstore.

Traveler motioned both of his friends back. He held a forefinger to his lips. He entered the building through what once was the front entrance. Now it was nothing more than a gaping tear in the structure.

Orwell followed him, guiding Traveler in the direction of the homing signal. The small wristband's pulsations grew stronger and stronger, quicker and quicker. Finally one steady beam of light emerged from the band. Traveler drew his knife and tensed his body to pounce.

He flicked on the flashlight and shone it into a bombed-out corner.

A pair of terrified eyes glared back at the torch.

Traveler exhaled sharply. "Shit."

Encircled in a glare of the flashlight was a young, dark-haired woman.

She was very young, very frightened, and very, very pregnant.

5

The woman regarded the three men before her with a mixture of fear and resignation. The stocky man in fatigues glared at her, obviously displeased. The large black man was clearly bemused. But the wiry one, the one with the headband and the steel-blue eyes, was gazing at her differently. She couldn't be sure what he was thinking. There was suffering in his eyes but strength as well, a strange combination of sympathy and resentment.

He folded his arms across his sleeveless black undershirt.

"No sign of a homing device."

Orwell passed a thick wrist over the woman. The wristband he wore emitted a steady, high-pitched wail. A light remained lit as he moved his arm above the woman. "Five will get you ten it's a surgical implant. Nonmutant slaves are hard to come by. When they run, they run *far*. They're valuable enough to track down and recapture. No owner will run the risk of a slave shaking loose of a regular bug."

Traveler agreed with a grunt. He observed the woman curiously.

"What are we going to do with her?" Hill asked.

"We can fit her in the Meat Wagon," Traveler said dully, still gazing at the raven-haired woman. "No problem."

"No problem, hell," Hill said. "If we're going to get out of here alive, we're going to have to haul ass back to the border, Kiel. Lickity split."

Hill shook his head angrily as he looked at the woman. "How

are we going to make good time if we're worrying about some pregnant woman bouncing around in the back?"

"I'll drive," Traveler replied. "Don't sweat it."

Orwell chuckled to himself. "I remember how *you* drive." He laughed. He stared at the newest addition to the troupe. "Lady, you're almost safer walking. This is the only man to drive a jeep halfway up a palm tree while doing the speed limit."

The woman allowed herself a small grin. Traveler smirked. Hill merely sighed in exasperation. "This isn't funny, guys. We're looking at Pope Gordy's big obsession here. If we take her along with her electric personality lighting up the airwaves with that homing signal, we're going to have both the Glory Boys *and* those mad monks on our butts. We're not equipped to handle that."

"We'll handle it," Traveler said.

Hill strode over to the spot where Traveler was crouched. "Talk sense, Kiel! We're jeopardizing everything here! Has being out in the desert sun fried your brain?"

Before he could get out another sentence, Hill found himself lifted by the armpits, staring into Traveler's icy blue eyes. The kind of eyes you didn't fuck with. Hill hadn't even seen the man stand, let alone grab hold of him.

"My brain is as good as my reflexes," Traveler said. He let Hill back down onto his feet. "We'll handle it."

Orwell decided to ignore the entire altercation. He faced the young woman again. "The thing was, once we were up that tree, he decides to pop the jeep in reverse. Man. You never saw a tree get pruned quicker in your life."

Traveler walked over to the woman and knelt before her. Her eyes were large and green, her skin the color of cocoa. "Maria," he said, "we're not going to harm you. We know that Gordon is hunting you and we know why. My name is Traveler. This is Orwell and the man with the constant whine is named Hill. Can you understand me? Can you understand English?"

Maria nodded slowly.

Traveler smiled. "Good. Can you speak English?"

Maria nodded affirmatively, then catching herself, shook her head back and forth in a negative motion.

"Great." Hill smirked. "We have ourselves a half-wit."

The woman began to sob silently. She opened her mouth. No sound emerged.

Traveler leaned forward. "You can't speak English."

Maria sobbed silently. She formed a scissor motion with her right hand and and jammed it down into her mouth. Traveler gently took her chin in the palm of his hand and, with his thumb, prodded her mouth open. She allowed this, forming an oval shape with her lips. Traveler pointed the flashlight down her throat.

Her tongue had been cut out.

Orwell, gazing over his shoulder, allowed himself a heartfelt "God damn."

Traveler flicked off the light and took her by the hand. "Did Gordon do this to you?"

The woman nodded. Traveler helped her to her feet. "We're going to get you out of here."

Hill muttered something under his breath.

Traveler took Maria by the arm and led her out of the drugstore. He walked her toward the restaurant down the street, where the Meat Wagon was still hidden. "Rest for a few hours. Then we'll leave."

Hill and Orwell trailed behind them. "Shit," Hill hissed into the night. "Kiel is going soft, man. He would never have jeopardized a misson because of some half-breed bitch and her kid. Damn. I don't understand it."

Orwell shrugged his massive shoulders. "He hasn't gone soft, Hill. You know that. He has his reasons. We all have our private demons to wrestle with. You, for instance, have a mouth that won't quit."

"Hey, I only say what I feel."

"Keep it up and you're going to be feeling someone's hands around your neck. Then you won't be saying or feeling nothing much at all."

"Jesus," Hill muttered. "What ever happened to democracy?"

"It got blown up on December twentieth, 1989," Orwell reminded him.

The two men followed Traveler back into the restaurant in silence.

Traveler turned to his companions. "Might as well sack out for three hours. We're going to have some hard riding ahead of us."

Traveler gave Maria his sleeping bag.

"What are you going to be doing?" Hill asked Traveler.

Traveler walked out the back door of the restaurant. "I'll get the Meat Wagon ready."

Hill was going to tell him that the Meat Wagon *was* ready but decided not to. Orwell smiled to himself. Hill placed a finger to his Adam's apple. No use taking chances on it getting squashed prematurely.

Within minutes the three were asleep.

Traveler siphoned the fuel from the VW's vinyl wading pool into an inflatable fuel bladder in the back of the Meat Wagon. The Wagon housed a fifty-gallon fuel tank that would, under ideal conditions, allow the vehicle to travel 1,400 miles before refueling. The bladder held an extra forty or fifty. No telling how crazy the ride back to the States would be. It would pay to have an extra margin of safety.

Traveler checked the booby traps on the car. They were all working. They were designed to keep outside scavengers on the outside. Since explosives would damage the car as well as a potential car thief, the traps were spring-and-tension guerrilla warfare concoctions.

The back of the Meat Wagon housed a small refrigerator, a cot, and a food locker. Traveler took the canned goods and the bottled water he had scavenged and stored in the VW and loaded them into the tear-shaped vehicle.

He checked the weapons rack. Two Heckler and Koch HK91 heavy assault rifles stood gleaming, replete with three boxes of ammo. These little babies could penetrate trees, cars, and brick walls with no sweat.

In a pouch next to the refrigerator were three four-pointed steel stars, some three and a half inches in diameter. Ninja *shuriken*: When hurled at high speed by someone trained in the martial arts, their razor-sharp points could slice through flesh effortlessly. Traveler slipped them into a black leather band wrapped around his right wrist.

Three Armalite AR-180s, lighter than the HK91s but pretty accurate, were under the dash. Traveler reached into the glove compartment and found his battered Colt Government Model Mark IV .45 Caliber Pistol. He had left the pistol in the car, never expecting to need it again.

There was a rack for the 12-gauge riot shotgun and a small black case placed under the front seat. Traveler reached into the case and removed his mini-crossbow. It was the size of a sawed-off shotgun, complete with a thumb-hole pistol grip. Traveler picked up the weapon and grinned. He felt like a medieval gangster . . . again.

A year ago he had left most of this behind. He had thought he could get away from the fighting and the killing. He was wrong.

He didn't regret that error, however. Perhaps he had been sent back here for a purpose. A small eternity ago, when he was just a man—a career soldier by the name of Kiel Paxton—all he had wanted out of life was a home, a family. For a few short years he had been lucky.

He had married his high-school sweetheart. It had seemed the American thing to do. On April 26, 1985, a son was born. Kiel Junior. A little blue-eyed kid that was the spitting image of his pop. Everyone figured that he'd grow up and become a soldier just like Daddy.

But he never got the chance to grow up. Global insanity put an end to his life before his fifth birthday. When the missiles hit New York, nearby New Jersey was taken out as well: a flash, a roar, a firestorm.

Kiel never got the chance to rescue his wife and child from the madness of others. He was in a veterans hospital half a nation away when his family was wiped out.

He leaned against the Meat Wagon and loaded his crossbow. God damn it, maybe this time around he would manage to save a family.

It didn't matter much if it wasn't his family.

It was a family all the same.

He placed the crossbow next to the Meat Wagon and, under the baleful glow of the full moon, walked across the restaurant garden to the remains of a brick wall. Gritting his teeth, he pulled back his left fist and sent it hurtling, karate-style, into the solid surface. The bricks smashed. A shaft of pain shot up through his arm. He smashed the wall again and again and again. Gradually he no longer felt the pain.

By the time he was done, the man named Kiel Paxton was gone, buried under an avalanche of hurt and anger. The man

called Traveler, the mercenary, the killer, had taken his place.
The past was dead. The present was alive . . . for now.

Traveler felt a heartbeat behind him. He pulled out a Ninja
shuriken from his studded wristband and spun around, poised to
hurl it.

Standing in the entranceway to the restaurant was Maria, her
light-brown skin highlighted by the moon's gleam. She offered
Traveler a tentative smile. She had watched both men battle for
possession of a single self. She knew that neither had won a clear
victory.

She returned to her sleeping bag secure in the knowledge that
she would be protected by them both.

The man and the mercenary.

6

The Meat Wagon slipped out of the remnants of the town unnoticed . . . or so Traveler hoped. He sat behind the wheel, a portrait of determination. Orwell's massive frame was squeezed into the space next to the driver's seat, a cushionless area he shared with the weapons rack.

In the back, Hill sat sullenly next to a placid Maria.

"Where do you think we are?" Traveler asked.

"Not too far from Hermosilla," Orwell replied. "A couple of hundred miles away from the border."

"The area clear?" Traveler asked.

"Seemed okay," Orwell replied, "which made me suspicious. No scavengers, no roadrats, no nothing."

"Maybe the Glory Boys drove them away," Traveler suggested.

"There'd have to be one hell of a lot of 'em to do that," Orwell said with a grunt.

"Let's hope not."

Traveler hit the highway. The pavement before him was cracked and shattered. Every bump caused Maria to wince and hold her swollen body.

Traveler slowed down. "When do you think she's due?" he asked Hill.

Hill didn't bother to look at the sweating woman next to him. "Who do I look like, Marcus Welby?"

Traveler maneuvered the Meat Wagon around the Olympian

potholes in the road. Maria tried to hide her discomfort. She bit down on her lower lip so hard it bled.

"Aw, the hell with this," Traveler muttered. He pulled off the road, onto the desert floor, and, popping the Wagon into four-wheel drive, hit the sand. Traveler pushed the van forward—fifty, sixty, seventy miles an hour. He didn't want to push it too far because of the excess weight the Wagon was handling and the excess weight Maria was carrying.

The three men in the car were silent. There was something *wrong* about all this. There was nothing that could be discerned by the human eye. The desert seemed deserted enough. But this trio was composed of combat veterans. In combat, you lived by your intuition as much as your skills. They *felt* a danger outside the car, an unfocused, omnipresent threat.

Instinctively Traveler killed the lights on the Wagon. Relying solely on the illumination provided by the moon, he angled the auto northward. He hadn't been driving more than ten minutes when the Wagon inexplicably pitched forward. Maria groaned as she rolled over in the back of the van. Traveler wrenched the steering wheel hard to the right. But it was too late. The Meat Wagon stuck into the desert terrain like an arrow in a flaccid target.

"Man, I told you this was crazy," Hill muttered, clambering out of the van. "Taking a woman on the road with you is crazy. Plain and simple. Taking a pregnant woman on the road is just fuckin' idiocy."

Traveler and Orwell stood in front of the Meat Wagon.

"No real damage," Traveler surmised.

Orwell nodded, walking around the grille. "Looks like we hit a pothole. We just fell in."

Traveler and Orwell slowly lifted the Wagon's nose and pushed it back two feet onto level ground.

Traveler stared at the hole in the middle of the desert they had hit. It was no bigger than a city manhole. "I'm not an expert on environmental shit," Traveler said, "but holes appearing in sand strikes me as being a little odd."

Hill marched up to Traveler. "You're not going to go down there, are you?"

"No."

"Thank God."

"*We* are."

"Shit."

Orwell merely smiled as Traveler attached a climbing rope to the front fender of the Wagon and dropped it down the hole. He gazed into the blackness, following the rope's descent. "Doesn't seem too deep."

He tossed a heavy assault rifle over his shoulder and grabbed on to the rope. "Orwell, make sure Maria's all right. If you spot anyone heading in our direction, yell like hell, rev up the engine, and wait."

"Yes, sir."

Hill watched Traveler slither down the rope. He grabbed an Armalite 180 and slung it over his shoulder. "Don't tell me. I get to bring up the rear."

"History repeats itself," Traveler's voice said from the gaping hole in the desert.

Hill shinnied down the rope after his leader.

Traveler hit solid ground some fifteen feet below the hole. He squatted close to the earth and extended a hand.

"Concrete."

Hill dropped off the rope and landed at Traveler's side. "What is this, a cave?"

Traveler removed a small flashlight from his belt and shone it before him. He whistled softly between his teeth. The Meat Wagon had crashed through the roof of a desert storeroom. Traveler guided the light over a hangarlike space filled with hundreds of boxes.

"Look at this," Traveler whispered. "Food. Weapons. Jesus, they even have mortars."

"Looks like someone is preparing for a small war."

Traveler walked by the large crates marked ammunition. "There's nothing small about it," he replied. "Let's see how far this goes."

The two men walked down a darkened corridor. Traveler snapped off the torch. "There's light up ahead."

Hill nodded. "I hear voices too."

The two men made their way to the end of the dark passageway. They peered around a rough concrete curve. Neither man could believe what they saw.

Before them, illuminated by dull electric lights, was an underground city, crudely constructed but well equipped. A few Glory Boys patrolled the area. The place was made even eerier by the fact that the caverns housing the city seemed to be lined with metal.

"Well, that explains why the desert was cleared out when we drove down here," Hill whispered. "These Glory Boys probably ran everyone off."

"Look at that," Traveler said, pointing to a large ramp. "That's big enough to drive trucks down."

"How the hell did they build these things?"

"It might not have taken them too long. I think that maybe before the war this was some sort of oil refinery. The shells of the tanks form the caverns. They just pushed the tanks together and welded passageways from tank to tank."

"It would take an awful lot of work to bury them under the desert."

"Who knows?" Traveler shrugged. "Maybe the work was done before the war. Maybe it was a squatters' camp. Maybe the war took care of placing the desert on top of the tanks."

The two men's conversation was cut short by three short horn bursts.

Traveler turned and ran back down the darkened corridor. "The Meat Wagon. Let's go."

He could hear the sound of distant gunfire as he climbed back up the rope. He clambered topside, Orwell extending a mammoth hand to pull him to safety.

"What's going on?" Traveler shouted.

"I have good news and bad news," Orwell replied. "One: Our little mama is having contractions. Two: There's a few hundred Glory Boys making a beeline for us as we speak."

Traveler stared into the murky night. Orwell had called it. Glory Boys on horseback, in jeeps and transport trucks were rushing toward them.

Hill ran toward the Wagon. "Let's blow, Kiel."

Orwell climbed into the Wagon. Maria was in the back. She was chewing on a piece of rope to help her get through the pains. "It'll be all right, Mama." Orwell smiled. "Things will get better as soon as we move out."

Traveler slid behind the steering wheel. Hill was at his back. "Peel out, Kiel. Let's put some miles between us and them."

"We can't peel out," Traveler said from between clenched teeth. "We might hurt the baby."

Hill rolled his eyes. "What do you think the Glory Boys will do to the baby? Wrap it in swaddling clothes?"

Bullets began zinging off the van's armor. Traveler stared at the desert before him. There was no way he could outrun them with a pregnant woman in the back of the van. There was no way three men could hold them off either.

He glanced into the back of the Wagon. Maria was trying to hide her pain. Orwell was cradling a heavy assault rifle, his face a mask of determination. Hill was simply pissed off. He was going to die over a wetback baby and he didn't like it.

Traveler suddenly smiled. Hill gave him a fish-eyed look. Without saying a word, Traveler reached past the weapons rack and pulled out a small satchel he had taken out of the restaurant/ bar and placed into the Wagon earlier. He removed two large metal pipe bombs filled with urea nitrate, an explosive that was, literally, half piss.

Traveler held the pipes in his left hand. Let's hear it for survivalist mentality, he thought. He lit the fuses and dropped the two bombs into the pothole leading to the underground ammo storage dump.

Hill couldn't resist laughing. "I don't believe you!"

Traveler slowly accelerated. He sent the Meat Wagon tooling off into the desert night at a jaunty twenty miles an hour. The Glory Boys behind him, sensing a kill, lunged forward as one. Traveler picked up his Heckler-Koch and grinned. He had a sixty-second fuse on those things.

Hill and Orwell, without having to be told, grabbed their rifles and placed the muzzles in the gun slits on the back of the van.

They waited.

Behind them, five hundred screaming right-wing extremists charged, willing to eliminate four innocent people and a Wankel engine for the love of God, country, and personal advancement.

Imagine their surprise as the desert rose up to meet them. Traveler laughed out loud (the first time in years) as a double-faced roar shook the heavens. The desert was illuminated from below as the few hundred horses, the fifty jeeps, and the two dozen troop transports passed over the ammo storage center.

A grainy volcano erupted from the desert, pulverizing the advancing troops.

Metal, wood, grit, and random debris cut down the endless line of paranoid patriots. There was nothing to grab onto, the Glory Boys found, in a situation where the earth met the sky with a surprising sense of determination.

"Open fire, boys," Traveler said flatly.

Hill and Orwell licked their lips in anticipation as the dust cleared and the few dozen survivors of the manmade inferno staggered out of the cataclysm.

Within seconds five hundred living, breathing human animals had been slaughtered.

And for what?

Traveler propelled the Meat Wagon forward into the endless night. He had never enjoyed killing. He had never gotten used to the presence of death. To take a single life was an act of enormous consequence. In one moment an *active* object, a being capable of movement, emotion, and thought, became something as exhilarating as a piece of lawn furniture.

Traveler took killing personally.

That could have made him a fourth-rate mercenary.

Instead it made him a first-class human being.

He raised his right hand and tilted the rearview mirror to the van. Maria was silently sobbing, the rope still clenched between her teeth. Traveler tried to absolve himself of his sins. At least her baby was safe. Hill and Orwell continued to fire, well after the point where their ammunition was effective. Traveler didn't utter a word. Let them take out their frustrations on the living dead.

Traveler continued heading north. He had overcome a major hurdle in their odyssey. How many more remained before him?

The answer was not long in coming.

He shook his head and sighed as he caught sight of a manmade dust storm on the ridge ahead.

Horsemen. Jeeps. Long black robes blotting out the stars.

As if on command, the sky burst into flame.

One hundred flaming crosses blocked the Meat Wagon's path.

Traveler had just knocked out a major portion of a vindictive army to save the life of a single soon-to-be-child.

How would he handle a group of religious fanatics whose single goal in life was to prevent it from being born?

He didn't stop to think about it. He hit the gas and propelled the Meat Wagon forward into a collision with the future.

7

The flaming crosses danced in the darkness around the Meat Wagon, eventually surrounding the vehicle. Traveler slowed the van down.

"What are you doing?" Hill demanded.

"Thinking," Traveler replied. He couldn't just plow through them without causing injury to Maria and her child.

There were two machine-gun turrets on the Wagon's roof but they didn't seem operable. One of the guns was pretty mashed up. The other looked like it had collected a dozen years' worth of rust in that many months. Mowing the monks down was out of the question.

Traveler attempted to buy some time. If he could stall the horde, give them a nice line of snappy patter, perhaps they'd relax their stance. He could drive through, get the monks behind them, and allow Hill and Orwell to open fire in a strafing action.

He brought the Meat Wagon to a complete halt. He allowed the engine to idle.

The only sound to be heard was the soft, guttural noises Maria was making.

"How's she doing?" Traveler asked no one in particular, keeping his eyes on the crosses before him.

"The contractions are getting closer together," Orwell said. "We might be godfathers soon."

"Great," Hill muttered.

Traveler couldn't argue that point. Rotten timing. Very rotten timing.

The line of crosses before the van grew closer. Traveler fought back a sudden wave of fear as he watched the monks ride closer. It was a sight straight out of a nightmare. Pale-skinned men in midnight robes, carrying burning spears and automatic weapons, all astride frothing, sweating steeds. The moonlight caused their elongated shadows to twist and turn toward the van. Traveler watched as a lone rider spurred his horse onward. If this wasn't an insight into hell, nothing was.

The leader of the group rode forward. It wasn't the pope. It wasn't Gordon. Traveler scratched his chin slowly. Some things never changed. When there was fighting to be done, the fearless leaders, the fools who processed their young men into cannon fodder, usually remained at the back of the line, safe and sound.

The lead monk stopped some twenty feet from the van. He had a greasy black beard and half a mouthful of teeth. He flashed the occupants of the van a wolfish grin. He looked like the poster boy from a harmonica company.

"We've come for the woman," the monk declared. "We have you surrounded."

"That I can see," Traveler shouted back from within the Wagon. "But we have no woman. Sure wish we did. Traveling can get lonely."

The monk grinned again.

Traveler continued, "There are three of us here. All men. Two of my friends from the States came down here looking for me. I've been lost in the desert. They found me in a town a few miles back. We're heading back north."

The monk glanced behind him at his men. They all smirked in unison. Traveler glanced in the rearview mirror. The line of horsemen behind the van was slowly advancing. He'd have to play this one by ear.

"There's no reason we should fight," Traveler called. "You have the advantage, no doubt about that, but a lot of you will die trying to capture us."

"True," the monk said. "It would be senseless to battle if the woman was not in your auto."

Silence.

The monk threw his flaming spear into the desert. The cross continued to burn, giving the monk a supernatural glow. "But if the woman *is* in your auto—"

"I told you she wasn't."

The monk slid down off his horse. "Then you will have no objection to my looking for myself."

Traveler remained in the car. "No one touches my wheels but me or my friends," he declared.

The monk continued to move forward. The horses behind him followed. "I demand to see the interior of your van in the name of the God of the Nouveau Testament and by the power of Pope Gordon I, Leader of the Right to a Good Life Church."

"And I refuse in the name of Traveler and the power of a rifle big enough to turn you and your horse into Alpo before you can even raise that popgun you're carrying."

The monk glanced at the light assault rifle in his right hand. The monks around the Meat Wagon seemed shaken. The word "Traveler" could be heard whispered in the night.

Traveler watched the monk hesitate.

His hand moved toward the gearshift. He tried not to look at any of the faces of the other monks in front of the van. He wanted them to remain anonymous. That made things easier. That made sleeping simpler.

He whispered, "Hold on to Maria," and smacked his hand down on the gearshift. The Meat Wagon sprang forward, like a pouncing jungle cat, sending up a spray of sand and grit in its wake. The horses behind the vehicle reared, their surprised riders hanging on for dear life.

Dear life was something the leader of the monk mob lost as soon as the van careened forward. Traveler hit the bearded man head on. There was a creaking noise, a scream and tumbling thud from both below and atop the vehicle as the van sliced the armed marauder in two.

The horsemen in front of the car scattered as the Meat Wagon headed up a large sand dune. Automatic fire crackled from all around Traveler as the holy men opened up at the retreating auto.

The van careened forward, its four-wheel drive allowing it to dig into the swirling grit.

Bullets sizzled past the Meat Wagon, pummeling its exoskeleton like deadly raindrops.

"Return their fire, god damn it," Traveler hissed to Hill and Orwell behind him. "They're going to turn this van into Swiss cheese."

"But—" Hill began.

"Return their fire, god damn it!"

Orwell and Hill stuck their rifle barrels through the firing slits in the back of the van and began pounding the advancing monks. Five. Ten. Twenty men down immediately. Gradually the monks began to fall back.

Traveler sent the Meat Wagon hurtling up the sand dune. When it reached the top, he allowed the van to roll to a halt. He turned and faced the two men.

"What are they doing?"

"They've stopped," Orwell breathed, his dark faced covered with sweat. He wore a strange, haunted expression on his face. "They're just waiting at the foot of the dune."

Traveler nodded. "They'll never be able to make it on those plugs they're riding. They're stuck down there. They can't charge straight up."

Neither Hill nor Orwell said a word. Within a second, he saw why. Maria was on her back. She had been hit in the worst place, the most painful place someone in combat could be hit. It was the center of fear, of anger, of hunger and even love. True soldiers lived on their guts and prayed they'd never take a gut wound.

The bullets must have entered the van through one of the slits in the rear. She must have been watching the monks giving chase. The two bullets had hit her in the stomach, making wounds no larger than dimes. Traveler could have put his fist through the exit wounds in her back, though. They were large and jagged. The interior of the van was splattered with blood.

She had never uttered a sound when she was hit.

But, then again, she couldn't have, could she? Gordon had taken care of that.

Traveler stared at the wide-eyed girl, lying in a pool of crimson liquid littered with skin and white cartilage.

Something within him snapped. He reached over to the weapons rack and removed his HK91. He took two extra clips of ammunition and stuck them in his belt. The rifle fired the standard U.S. military caliber, and 7.62 NATO cartridge. It was one of the most powerful pieces of weaponry around before the war.

In the right hands, it was exceedingly accurate.

Traveler got out of the car, rifle in hand.

"Kiel," Hill whispered, "are you nuts?"

Hill made an effort to pull Traveler back into the van. Orwell put out a restraining hand. "Let him be," he advised.

Traveler pulled the rifle's charging handle, putting a cartridge under the hammer.

He had been a fool to risk the girl's life. He had expected a miracle. Now his mouth tasted of sand. This was a world without hope, a world without magic, a world without miracles.

He stood at the top of the sand dune. Seventy or eighty of the armed monks gathered at the foot of the hill.

"You have killed the woman," Traveler yelled.

The monks let out a cheer, waving their rifles and their burning spears in the air.

"Now," Traveler said softly, "you'll pay for it."

He opened up, gritting his teeth and tensing his body against the reverberations of the gun.

The monks had been caught by surprise. They didn't return the fire. They reined their horses in, trying desperately to turn and gallop off in the opposite direction. Traveler slowly marched down the sand dune, firing. He didn't falter. He didn't hesitate. His aim was sure and true. His feet never lost their hold on the cascading sand.

The air was shattered by the screams of dying men and the cries of frightened animals. The flaming crosses tumbled through the air, landing on the ground beneath the frightened marauders. A few monks passed too close to their torches. Their robes ignited. They didn't suffer too long from the flames, however. The HK91 tore them to shreds, putting them out of their misery almost before they experienced it. Traveler didn't remember changing clips even though he must have done it several times.

Within minutes, the air reeked with the stench of burned flesh, urine, and blood. It was a thick, musty smell. The smell of death. A smell that would stay in this place a long time.

Hill and Orwell stood on the top of the dune next to the Meat

Wagon and watched the lone gunman calmly march into the wall of flame and flesh.

The rifle bellowed a staccato tune and Traveler continued his march.

Hill and Orwell exchanged frightened glances. "That's fucking spooky, man," Hill hissed. "He's gone over the top."

Orwell shook his head sadly. "No, he hasn't. He's just gone back in time."

For a split second, Traveler was once again Lt. Kiel Paxton, well-seasoned LURP—member of the Long Range Reconnaissance Patrol units, guys gonzo enough to make the Green Berets look like Campfire Girls.

He was a soldier in a foreign land, firing blindly into the jungles, trying to stay alive. Trying to kill anything that might possibly pose a threat.

Within three minutes every one of the monks was dead. Their torches still spat out flames, strewn about on the desert floor. Traveler, dazed and angry, still seeing the dead woman in the back of his van, walked from body to body, firing point blank into the bloodied robes of the monks.

Hill and Orwell walked slowly back into the van.

"Hey," Orwell said. "Look at this."

"Oh, Christ," Hill muttered, climbing into the vehicle after Orwell.

Traveler removed a spent clip and replaced it with a full one. He shot full blast into anything that resembled something that once was human.

The desert sky echoed with the *sput-sput-sputtering*. All was quiet. Traveler glanced at the top of the dune where the Meat Wagon was still idling. Orwell and Hill were nowhere to be seen. Traveler sighed and prepared to empty a few more rounds into the black-robed forms.

He was stopped by the presence of a strange sound.

He cocked his head.

An unfamiliar, high-pitched wailing wafted through the cold night air.

Traveler relaxed his grip on the trigger of the rifle. He shook his head as if recovering from an unexpected blow. He had heard that sound before. He remembered it from a few centuries ago. It took him a few seconds to place it.

He shook with a sudden spasm of laughter. A single tear ran down his face as he ran up toward the top of the sand dune and the waiting Meat Wagon.

Inside a baby was crying.

8

After much protesting, Hill was assigned the task of holding the small boy child while Orwell and Traveler dug a crude grave atop the sand dune where Maria had died.

The baby had almost literally burst from her womb minutes after her death. Orwell and Hill had to act quickly to keep the child alive. They cut the cord with their knives and bathed the child with precious water from their canteens. It hadn't cried long. It seemed to sense the solemnity of the occasion and lapsed into a thoughtful hush.

Traveler dug silently, using both his hands and an old combat boot to scoop away the sand. Tiny, irritating granules of the stuff rubbed the wrist raw beneath his wristband. Angrily Traveler unstrapped the studded band and tossed it toward the van. He then continued digging. Orwell, stripped to the waist, cupped his hands together, palms up, and pushed and prodded the grit, humming softly to himself.

A lullaby.

Hill held the newborn baby awkwardly in his folded arms, cradling it like it was a cross between a bobcat and an activated grenade. The child didn't squirm or cry out, a fact that made Hill even more irritable.

"There's something wrong with this kid," he groused. "It isn't crying. It's just staring at me."

"Maybe he thinks you're his mama—" Orwell began.

"Fuck you," Hill injected.

"And he's in *shock*." Orwell chuckled.

"Maybe he's a mutant or a retard or something," Hill replied.

Traveler stopped working and, staring at the portrait of the awkward Hill-as-Madonna with child, had to crack a lopsided grin. "If he keeps on staring at you, he *will* be retarded or something."

The baby twisted its head upon hearing Traveler's voice. The child had pale-green eyes and a shock of light-brown hair already neatly swirled atop his head. Traveler grinned at the baby. Traveler knew he had to be imagining it—the child was only an hour old—but he swore the baby grinned back. Those eyes. They seemed, somehow, *older* than any child's eyes he had ever seen before.

Traveler returned to his grim task. Then again, he hadn't really encountered many babies in the last fifteen or sixteen years. At least babies that looked like babies.

After a while, the grave was dug. Orwell and Traveler wrapped Maria's body in a blanket, tied the blanket closed, and lowered her body into the shallow hole.

Even Hill was moved by the scene. "Look, kid," he whispered to the child. "That's your mama. If you live and grow up and get old, always remember this. This was where your mama died. She died here. You were born here. Remember."

Hill walked up to the gravesite, babe still in arms. He joined Orwell and Traveler, staring at the mummylike figure.

"Are we going to say anything or just keep our mouths shut, silentlike?" Hill asked.

There wasn't too much silence on the hilltop. A small army of buzzards was fluttering down, screeching in delight, at the bottom of the sand dune, relishing every last morsel offered by the remains of the crusading monks.

The smell of burned flesh and the inhuman screams of the carrion eaters caused Traveler to shiver.

"It seems like such a waste," Orwell finally said. "Such a young, pretty girl. Not cut up. Not screwed up. She just wanted to be a mother. Doesn't seem fair."

Traveler looked up at the placid face of the baby boy. "It's not fair," he said. "But she *is* a mother. She did have a son. Now it's up to us to keep him alive, I suppose."

"Now, *that's* not fair," Hill injected. The baby in his arms laughed and swatted him good-naturedly on the nose. "Nobody asked you," Hill muttered. The child continued to laugh.

"Maybe that's the prayer she needs," Traveler said, staring at the corpse. "If there's a God, maybe he'll listen to a child before he'll pay attention to us."

Traveler looked toward the heavens. "Take this woman to a better place and help us take her baby to—" he glanced off into the postnuclear landscape—"a better future."

"Amen," Orwell muttered.

"Amen," Hill seconded.

The baby hit him in the nose again. "Somebody else want to hold him for a while?" Hill asked.

Traveler and Orwell began to cover the body, kicking sand down into the hole they had just finished digging. Their progress was halted by a deafening roar.

The three men looked up at once and were confronted by a wolf . . . or something whose ancestors might have been lupine before the big nuke-out. It was big, at least four feet tall and six feet long. It was furry, its boil-covered body laced with large clots of pus-stained gray hair. It had three eyes and saber teeth. It was staring at Maria's body hungrily.

It smelled of decayed flesh, dried dung, and spit.

"Am I awake or is that a nightmare?" Orwell hissed.

"Both," Traveler replied.

The two men stood, defenseless, next to the open grave. Both men had removed their weapons when they began digging. Hill, on the other hand, had a knife strapped to his boot. To retrieve the knife, however, he'd have to place the baby down on the desert sand. Hill stared at the wolf-mutant and then at the child. The kid wouldn't be more than an appetizer for the creature, but he was pretty sure it would spring for the baby should he give up his grip.

"Do you know any more prayers?" Orwell said to Traveler.

"Doesn't look like the first one is working," Traveler said. "Why try another?"

Traveler stared at the beast. Foul-smelling saliva poured out of the creature's mouth in a steady stream. The beast was aware of every movement the men made but its attention, for the most part, was focused on Maria's body. Traveler realized that. He was determined to keep the monster from feeding on this particular corpse.

The irony was inescapable. There were at least one hundred slightly char-broiled cadavers not three hundred yards away, yet this particular beast decided to pick Maria. Probably because she was the freshest, cleanest kill.

Traveler judged that the distance between himself and the creature was ten feet. He could easily toss a handful of sand into the creature's eyes and temporarily blind it. He'd gain maybe five or six seconds. But, then what?

He glanced sideways toward the Meat Wagon. His gun and crossbow were on the hood, a good fifteen feet away. He'd never make it. The creature, half-blinded and angry, would be on him in two good leaps.

The monster eyed the three men and the tidbit. Would they fight? Would they run? Would they join the meal?

He never got the chance to find out.

The creature opened its mighty jaw to bellow a roar of warning. Suddenly the roar was cut short and the monster's growl turned into a whine.

The pointed side of the six-foot spear burst, javelin-style, through the roof of the monster's mouth, sending a thick spray of blood and garbage onto the grave.

The monster fell over in a moan, shook four times, and then remained still. Traveler stared at the spear. There were ceremonial feathers on it.

"What the fuck?" Orwell said, staring out into the desert, over the body of the beast. A bizarre figure atop a large beast sat there placidly.

Traveler only smiled and shook his head as the fish-faced pseudo-Indian atop the buffalo nodded at him.

"Are you making a habit out of saving my ass?" Traveler asked.

Orwell and Hill were in shock.

Rat Du Bois chuckled out loud, his reptilian mouth forming a stiff grin. "Hoi, hoi, hoi. I'm savin' a boy, mama's little baby loves this nucleoid."

"What the fuck is that?" Hill asked.

"It's a buffalo," Du Bois answered, lapsing out of rhyme. "Ain't you ever seen no nickels?"

Du Bois climbed off the buffalo and approached the baby.

"Jerry Hall, he was so small, a rat could eat him, hat and all," he recited.

The baby stared solemnly at the fish-faced stranger.

Du Bois continued to approach. Orwell stiffened, tensing for trouble. Traveler restrained him, giving him an it's-okay glance.

"The man in the moon looked out of the moon, looked out of the moon and said, 'Tis time for all good babies on Earth to think about getting to bed.'"

Du Bois cackled softly. The baby blinked three times and then lapsed into a peaceful slumber. Hill stared uncomprehendingly into Du Bois's stiffened and scarred face. The fishman shrugged. "I have a way with kids. You can put him in the back of your truck now. He'll sleep for a while. Little sucker is tired."

Hill carried the baby to the Meat Wagon, every now and then glanced warily over his shoulder at the weird warrior. He patted the child protectively as he placed him in the van.

Traveler smiled at the feathered rider. "Hill, Orwell, this is Rat Du Bois. He's a warrior of sorts."

Du Bois executed a small bow. "Warrior. Wanderer. Beggarman. Thief. Wizard. Warlock and rider of beef."

Orwell turned to Traveler. "Does he always talk like that?"

"It takes some explaining," Traveler acknowledged.

Du Bois reached into a deerskin satchel around his waist and produced a hefty packet. He tossed it at Traveler. "Here. You'll need this to keep the kid alive."

"What is it," Traveler said, "some herbal tonic?"

"It's formula, daddy," Du Bois replied with a smirk. "You mix it with water. Picked some up at that drugstore you vacated last night."

He shrugged, walking toward his buffalo. "Then again, maybe you won't want to keep the kid alive."

"And why the hell not?" Hill demanded, suddenly angry.

"You already got the Glory Gang on your buns. Keep the kid and you'll have more of those Crusaders than you can imagine chasing you as well."

Hill bit his lip. "That's our problem."

Traveler and Orwell exchanged smirks as Du Bois climbed atop his steed. "That it is. See you on the free side of the border, daddy-o's. *If* you make it."

Du Bois gave Hill two sharp jabs with his moccasined feet.

The creature turned around and shambled off into the night, Du Bois cooing softly. "Hark, hark! The dogs do bark! Beggars are coming to town. Some in jags and some in rags and some in velvet gowns."

Hill ran up to Traveler. "Is that guy for real?"

Traveler shrugged. "I'm no judge of that. He *is* right, though. We're going to have a rough time heading for the border."

"Do you think the kid is worth the risk?" Orwell asked. "Maybe Hill was on to something before. We could make a lot better time with just the three of us to consider."

"Never mind what I said before," Hill snapped. "We have a—a responsibility now. Don't you have any soul?"

The burly black man only laughed. "Just trying to be democratic, that's all."

"Well, I vote we get out of here as soon as possible," Traveler said, heading toward the Meat Wagon. "Like now."

He got into the van and cranked it down the far side of the dune, heading north. "My ears are buzzing," he said. "Someone must be talking up a storm about us right now."

A shiver shot through his body. Fuck a storm. It was more like a hurricane that was being formed around them.

9

Pope Gordon I, exalted leader of the Church of the Right to a Good Life, was not pleased. His hemorrhoids were acting up. He had a large, running sore on his neck that would not heal, and Brother Sanchez had just brought him a little bit of bad news. Maria, the servant girl, was dead. So were one hundred of Gordon's flock.

The baby—the one Gordon had been warned about—had escaped with his life, guarded by three renegade mercenaries.

The presence of mercenaries worried Gordon. He had been one himself. He had used that position to build himself a small empire before the war, journeying to fight in oil-rich countries on the side of the monied. They paid well—sometimes with their lives.

Gordon twisted his massive body around under the long, off-white cassock he wore. He had been younger then. Thinner. He fingered the boil on his neck. In better health too.

Gordon sat in the nearly destroyed Catholic church, on a wooden throne atop what once had been an altar. Shattered plaster statues of the saints surrounded him. Most of the statues had been smashed above the knees, the victims of target practice, giving the tableau an eerie touch. Gordon was being attended to by some of the holiest pairs of feet and ankles in Christian history.

"Brother Sanchez," Gordon said sweetly. "I am very disappointed in you."

"Me?" the cowled figure said, trembling. "I mean, yes, your Holiness. But why are you disappointed in me? I merely discovered what had happened."

"And you did nothing?" The pope gazed over Sanchez's shoulder. A small group of scowling monks had entered the church and stood in a single line in the last pew.

Gordon smiled. He loved performing before a crowd.

Sanchez was getting nervous. "No, your Holiness. There was nothing I could do. I was alone, on point, scouting the area. I discovered the massacre and ran back to my coven. We then came directly to you. The damage had already been done before I left. I swear. We saw the tire tracks leading away from the site but had no idea of what was going on."

"You had a good idea by the time you reached me, brother."

"Well, yes. That's true. On the way back we ran across a group of Glory Boys who were searching for three mercenaries who had blown up a Glory depot. They gave us a description and a name, Traveler. We assumed that these men also were responsible for our own setback."

Gordon nodded. "You are sure that the woman is dead?"

"Yes, your Holiness. We followed the impulse from the homing device to a grave on a hillside. We dug it up. She was there. The baby was not. She had given birth but there was only one body. We were going to carve up the body when the devil himself appeared astride a large woolly creature.

"The devil howled at us. The creature roared. It was a vision from hell, your Bigness."

Gordon sighed. Perhaps he had used the religious mumbo-jumbo a little too heavily in training his troops. They weren't very bright and were, perhaps, too impressionable. He shook his head and smiled sadly at Sanchez. Still, they were good fighters and the religion scare kept them in line.

Maybe even Gordon was letting the superstitious side of things rattle him. After all, what harm could this child do? It was an infant. Gordon was a man of the world. He had seen what happens to people who cling to various exotic religious beliefs. They lose their spontaneity. They lose their will to conquer, their will to survive at all costs.

Gordon believed in no god. He believed in nothing that he couldn't touch, hold, scratch, or claw. Still, that old priest seemed so *sure* of himself when he made that prophecy in his dying breath. Maybe it was just bullshit.

Well, it wouldn't hurt to be careful. Killing an infant should be easy. Tracking the brat's three protectors even easier.

Gordon extended his heavily ringed right hand toward the frightened Sanchez. "Kiss them and vow your obedience."

"Oh, yes, your Holiness. Thank you. Thank you."

Sanchez dropped to his knees and crawled toward the obese leader. As he bent toward the pope's right hand, he caught a glimpse of the knife poised in Gordon's left one. He made a move to back away. Gordon's massive right hand grabbed hold of Sanchez's contorted face, effectively blocking his scream. Sanchez's eyes nearly burst from their sockets as he saw the sharp blade of the knife sweep up toward him. He felt nothing as the point slid into the soft flesh under his chin and up into his brain.

Nothing.

Gordon slid the blade out, wiped it clean on Sanchez's drooping shoulder, and then, allowed the body to fall free. Sanchez tumbled down the steps and landed at the plaster feet of St. Francis of Assisi. Gordon figured that the statue had been that of St. Francis because there was a tiny plaster bird looking admiringly up past the smashed knees at where the saint once had stood. St. Francis liked animals. Especially birds.

Gordon liked animals. Especially sheep. Things often got lonely on the road.

"Excuse me, your Holiness," a monk called from the back.

"Give Brother Sanchez a nice funeral, will you, John?" Gordon told to the bearded monk.

"Yes, your Holiness."

As Gordon got up to leave, Brother John repeated, "Your Holiness. . . ."

The pope looked angrily at the monk. "What? What?"

"We have visitors. Glory Boys. Captain Memphis and . . . some*one* else."

"What do they want? Send them away. I have no time for secular matters right now."

"I think you do," Captain Memphis said, appearing in the back of the church. "I think it's time we abolished the concept of the separation of church and state."

"And pray tell, why?" Gordon smiled, snuggling back down into his throne.

"Because if your three foster-fathers, who are our three rebels, make it north of the border to United States territory, Gordo, both our asses will be in permanent slings."

"Blasphemy!" Gordon roared.

Memphis marched briskly toward the altar. For the first time in years, Gordon actually felt fear. Memphis was a compact man, blond, crew-cut, with a body filled with shrapnel and anger. The tanned Glory Boy stopped two feet before the ersatz holy man and sneered at him.

"Look, Gordon," he whispered. "Let's cut the crap. You can use your religious flim-flam on your latino brothers, but don't try it on me. Your name is Gordon Peissler. You were a slimy son of a bitch wanted by about every international law organization before the war and, as far as I'm concerned, you're still a slug.

"But I don't give a shit. You want South America as your empire, fine. But my leader wants the United States back. That's our empire.

"This Traveler, this wanderer, has eluded us for years. He's a single man who fights like a small garrison. In the last twenty-four hours, he's wiped out a few hundred of both of our men. I don't know how he got here or why. But I do know that if he gets back north and rejoins the new President, Jefferson, he'll lead the new United States military down here and wipe both our slates clean."

Memphis glared at the pope. "Are you reading me on this, Gordo?"

The man who called himself the pope felt the sweat roll down the massive folds of stomach beneath his cassock. He forced a smile to appear on his face. "Why, Captain Memphis, the church has, historically, backed just and righteous causes. I see no reason why my flock cannot work side by side with your Glory Boys."

Memphis returned the smile. "Fine. Then I think it's time you met the leader."

Gordon's smile faded. "Scar? I didn't think he actually existed! I mean, well, you know, we hear rumors and . . ."

"I exist, all right, Peissler," came a cracked voice from behind Gordon, "although I'm not the dashing figure I once was."

Gordon spun around, nearly toppling from his makeshift throne. Behind him, in a walker, was a skeletal figure clad in a charcoal-gray suit. He hobbled forward slowly, dragging a dead leg and a mangled arm. Half his face bore an expression of calm reserve, the dignified face of a man in his eighties. The other half was a mass of moist crimson red and purple scar tissue. Flashburn. The man had been too close to a nuclear explosion.

The pope stumbled to his feet. "Scar?"

The half-face emitted a harsh, cackling laugh. His good side broke into a grin. The scar tissue simply bubbled up and down where the mouth must have been before it was fused shut.

"Yes, *Scar*. A name some of your own people came up with when they first spotted me a year ago. Nice people. Not too bright."

Scar extended his good hand, balancing his withered one on the walker. "Mr. Peissler. I've heard so much about you."

Gordon grasped the bony hand. "And I, you, Scar."

The skeletal figure emitted a soft chuckle. "Please, Mr. Peissler. We are above the superstitious nonsense associated with this area. If we are going to work together, fight together, we should be honest with each other. You may call me by my correct name: Andrew Frayling . . . rightful President of the United States of America."

Gordon's mind went into overdrive. Andrew Frayling was the idiot of a President who merrily led the United States into the final world war way back when. A former Western movie star with an overdeveloped sense of macho and an underdeveloped mind, he played shootout with the world as the booty. Nobody won. Nobody.

Up until last year, Frayling roamed around the bombed-out plains of America, capturing cities and forcing them to pledge allegiance to his idea of America. Frayling's merciless Glory Boys killed all those who weren't patriotic enough.

But Frayling's base in Nevada had been blown to smithereens a year or so ago. Nuked, as a matter of fact. Frayling and his aides were supposed to have perished in the blast. A blast set off by . . .

Gordon blinked several times as the enormity of the situation began to hit him. *Traveler* had set off the blast. The Road Ghost was what the locals called him, a speeding spirit who eluded capture by all foolish enough to want to try.

The Road Ghost was back to haunt Frayling in a big way . . . and the President was asking Gordon to join him in a deadly military exorcism.

Frayling continued to pump the pope's hand. "Heh. Heh. Heh. Reports of my death have been widely exaggerated, Mr. Peissler . . . although, as you can see, cosmetically, I have been altered in a haphazard way. Please. Please," Frayling said, withdrawing his hand. "Sit down. Relax. I'll remain standing, if you don't mind. When I sit, I have a hard time getting to my feet again."

Gordon sank into his throne. The skeletal Scar remained at his walker. "Mr. Peissler, I will be brief. I am a dying man. I was caught in a blast last year, set off by unscrupulous traitors. They thought they killed me. They were wrong. They killed my aides. They killed my bodyguards. But me? I survived in an underground bunker.

"However, it is obvious that the blast had its effects on me. I grow weaker each day, Mr. Peissler. Before I die, however, I want to catch those traitors. I want to watch them tortured. I want them to beg me for a quick death."

Scar twisted his face into a grotesque grin. "On a more pressing level, these three outlaws are heading toward the United States. If they reach the border, they will no doubt assemble a large army of traitors led by a roadrat named Jefferson. They are well armed, Mr. Peissler. If they invade Mexico, there will be no stopping them.

"Now, the only thing slowing down our traitors' escape is the presence of a small child. A baby boy. Apparently, for reasons unbeknownst to me, they are caring for this child. Rumor has it you want the baby. I, on the other hand, want the scum traveling with the child.

"These traitors are wild, ruthless, and very inventive. Both of us have experienced the deadly extent of their creativity during the last day. I figure it is in our mutual interest to pursue this entourage jointly.

"Your men are excellent guerrilla fighters. My men possess solid military minds and a good deal of armaments. Many of your people know the desert. Many of mine know the area closest to the border. Between the two of us, we should be able to wipe these bastards off the face of the Earth forever."

Scar nodded at Gordon. "And, who knows? After I resume my rightful role as leader of the great United States, why couldn't I declare South America as a single nation . . . with one Gordon Peissler as Supreme Commander?"

Gordon found himself laughing out loud. He couldn't believe it. Gordon Peissler, mercenary turned religious zealot, was actually talking one on one with the President of the United States! Not only that but the President was practically promising Gordon a continent!

Gordon raised his right hand and made the sign of the cross in the air before Scar. "May the God of the Right to the Good Life bless our efforts, President Frayling."

"Amen," Scar said.

Three monks entered and dragged the body of Brother Sanchez off St. Francis's plaster feet. The tiny bird was now covered with blood.

Gordon watched as Sanchez was carted off. He coughed uncomfortably. "These old churches can be dangerous," he explained lamely. "Things are falling all the time."

"Yes." Scar nodded. "I never went to church a lot. I knew the people would understand. After all, I was their President. I was vulnerable even in the house of . . . The Man Upstairs. I figured He would understand too. After all, one leader to another. I did go to church once, though. Things were tough. I prayed for an hour."

He sighed and glanced at the pope with his one good eye. "The next day, the world blew up. Go figure."

10

The Meat Wagon barreled across the desert in the glaring noonday sun. Traveler, behind the wheel, fought off the dizziness caused by the merciless temperature. It must have been 120 degrees in the shade. The problem was, there wasn't any shade to be found.

Orwell fought drowsiness, clinging to the rifle while peering out the back of the van for any sight of possible pursuers.

Hill sat cross-legged and gazed at the sleeping child at his feet. "Maybe we should pull over and strike camp until nightfall," he said. "I don't like the kid just lying there. Maybe there's something wrong with him or something. Maybe it's the heat. Maybe—"

"You're beginning to sound like a mother." Traveler smirked, continuing to send the Meat Wagon sailing over the swirling sand.

"Fuck you."

"We should rest, though," Traveler admitted. "The Wagon's close to overheating and we don't have the water to spare."

Traveler pulled the Wagon to a halt. The three men out a tarp and made a makeshift tent, shielding them from the rays of the sun.

Hill removed the child from the back of the van. The child's forehead was covered with sweat. Hill daubed it off with a fingertip. "Poor kid," he muttered. "It was like an oven in there, Kiel."

The baby fluttered his eyelids and stared directly at Hill. Hill winced under the scrutiny. There was something *weird* about this baby. It seemed so serious. Maybe it was just the heat. Yeah. That could be it.

Traveler picked up his crossbow and, grabbing a shovel and a piece of tarp, set up a separate campsite some thirty feet away. He dug a hole in the sand large enough for him to squat in comfortably, snuggled up into it, and pulled the tarp above him. Within a few minutes a thin covering of blowing sand had gathered on the tarp, rendering him all but invisible. If anyone spotted the Meat Wagon and headed for it, Traveler would catch the movement from his vantage point and sound the alarm in time.

He hoped.

The relentless heat, the claustrophobic effect of the sand, and the strange, smothering caress of the constant breeze caused Traveler to slip into slumber.

He immediately began to dream. He was standing in a tower, a wooden observation tower. The tower was buffeted by large waves. Traveler leapt feet first from the swaying structure and landed in a place that was alien yet familiar.

It was a city . . . a city straight out of a storybook, straight out of a time every child had longed for. The buildings were white and majestic, almost Greek or Roman. Toga-wearing citizens, their faces unsullied by lines of alarm or sorrow, strolled casually along the streets.

Exotic birds flew across blue skies. Unicorns grazed on fields of brilliant green. Traveler was beside himself with happiness. This was Earth. He knew it. Yet, somehow, it was an Earth different from any history book had ever reported. It was . . . paradise.

Suddenly the sky grew dark and brooding. A massive shadow blotted out the sun. Traveler had time to look up and see a titanic wave rise and smash down on the city. The tidal wave skidded into the buildings, smashing them into rubble and snatching them along in its wake.

The people had no time to scream as the water overcame them. Bodies were everywhere. The animals were gone.

Only Traveler remained, shaking an angry fist at the sky, screaming, "It's not fair. It's not fair."

Traveler awoke with a start. He shook himself clear of the

dream. It was more than a dream, however. It seemed like a memory.

At that precise moment, the baby began to cry. Traveler slowly rose from his hiding place and walked toward the Meat Wagon. It was late in the afternoon. He had slept for four hours or so. Bad move, militarily, but a necessary one.

He thought about that dream. He had never had such a vivid nightmare before.

A deafening drone brought him back to reality.

He glanced up as a shadow sliced across the sky.

Traveler grabbed his crossbow and made a beeline for the Meat Wagon as one of the biggest, meanest planes he had ever seen buzzed overhead.

It was a prop-driven job. Traveler couldn't be sure but it looked like a World War II fighter plane.

As he approached the Meat Wagon, he tried to figure out just who the hell was flying the thing.

He never finished the thought process.

The gas grenade erupted near his feet.

By the time he hit the ground, he was unconscious.

11

Traveler awoke to find himself, Hill, and Orwell tied securely outside the Meat Wagon. Darkness was falling. A large, imposing figure, clad in a black military jumpsuit and face-concealing goggles, sat on a collapsible stool in front of them. The figure held the baby in its arms.

"You're pretty damn foolish to be cartin' a newborn around in the fucking desert," the stranger said.

Traveler shook his head slowly from side to side. His head was still buzzing from the gas. "We're just trying to head north."

"Yeah." The stranger chuckled. "You and half the world, I reckon."

Hill and Orwell were now awake. They gaped at the stranger. "Who the hell is . . .?" Hill began.

"Half the world?" Traveler interrupted.

"Yeah. There's a regular army not fifty miles behind you boys. But I suppose you realize that."

The stranger placed the baby down on a blanket and, producing a large knife, walked toward the three captives. Traveler glared at the figure, who bent over and sliced the ropes off their wrists.

"Didn't mean to rough you up," the stranger said. "But you were getting close to my home turf. I don't like company much. I've tried to keep to myself for years now. Been successful until you blundered in."

The speaker lifted the goggles off the concealed face. Traveler was expecting to seen an old, wizened man. Instead he found himself staring at the face of an angel. A young girl with close-cropped blond hair.

"Veronica Hart's the name," the girl said, spitting a wad of sand out of her mouth. "This here is my home."

She pointed to a carefully concealed geodesic dome, covered with hand-layered sand and sitting not a hundred feet from where the van was parked. Traveler was amazed he hadn't noticed it before. It was a professional camouflage job.

Traveler extended a hand. "Glad to meet you. I'm Traveler and these are my friends, Hill and Orwell."

"What's the baby's name?" the woman asked, glancing at the boy.

The three men looked at each other sheepishly. They hadn't even thought to name the kid as yet.

"Don't tell me." Veronica laughed. "Kid ain't got no name, right?"

"Right," Traveler said.

"Well, you'd better hurry up and name him. If those Glory Boys catch up with you, I'll have to know what to put on the kid's tombstone."

"You're a real optimist," Traveler said with a smirk.

"Can't be," the woman replied, smiling. "I'm a survivor."

Traveler glanced behind the Meat Wagon. The massive fighter plane was sitting harmlessly in the sand. Veronica saw Traveler regard the plane with awe.

"Something, isn't it?" She smiled. "It's a four-engined B-seventeen G. Classic World War II bomber. Has thirteen fifty-caliber guns in its chin, nose, dorsal, center fuselage, ventral, waist, and tail positions. The engines are turbo-supercharged, so I can get up to thirty thousand feet up yonder before I conk out. Pretty impressive, eh?"

Traveler gaped at the woman. She couldn't have been more than twenty-five years old. "How did you learn how to fly one of these?"

"My daddy taught me," Veronica said with a shrug. "His daddy taught him."

Traveler rubbed his wrists gently, restoring the circulation. The woman sat down behind the gurgling baby. "Daddy worked for the government. He was a military man. But he got sick and tired of what was going on in the Pentagon with Frayling. He said that the country was collapsing from within." She looked up at Traveler with a narrow smile. "Of course he never figured on it blowing up and out."

Traveler nodded. "Not many people did."

"I think what irritated Daddy most was the cowardice involved. The military tried to cover up what they did by talking nonsense. Did you know that the State Department replaced the word 'killing' in their reports with 'unlawful or arbitrary deprivation of life'? No shit. They did.

"They came up with all kinds of words to make what they were doing sound better. They called peace 'permanent prehostility'; combat 'violence processing,' and civilian casualties in a nuclear war were called 'collateral damage.' Can you beat that?"

Traveler smiled thinly. He knew what she was talking about. He remembered reading, way back, about America invading a tiny joint named Grenada in the wee hours of the morning. Technically, it had been called a "predawn vertical insertion."

Veronica was laughing. "Daddy was something. He was always pissed off about how the Pentagon was advancing the science of fuzzistics, of not being clear about anything. Eventually they sent him down here—booted him down here, really—to head up this hush-hush military genetics research. Freaky shit. Then the big bang happened. We survived but a lot of the oil and chemical places north of here just went kablooie. Most of the genetic experiments busted their cages and headed for the hills, which, at that point, were popping up all around us."

"Christ," Traveler said. "It must have been hellish."

"You got that right." Veronica laughed. "The U.S. military had set up a lot of chem research facilities down here. When they went up, spewing out all that shit, they took most of the life, human and otherwise, out with it. For the first few years we lived here, we stayed pretty much in the dome. Later we wore oxygen masks when we *had* to go outside. Gradually the sky turned from yellow to blue and we started breathing any old junk that was in the air.

"The critters that made it through all this were pretty twisted. Lots of times they'd show up here for food. Lots of times they figured us to be their main course. Still, we survived. On the plus side, most of the locals consider this place accursed, a devils' stomping ground. That keeps most folks away. Visitors usually mean trouble of one kind or another. On the down side, conversation is pretty much a lost art around here. Daddy never really trusted strangers much. We always kept to ourselves. He died a year or so ago. Now I make my rounds solo. Protecting home and hearth and all that shit."

She got to her feet. "You guys better make time if you're going to outrun those Glory Boys."

Veronica bent down and picked up the baby. She walked over to the rising Traveler and handed him the child. "Take care of this kid too. He's a beaut. Most of the kids born hereabouts are pretty sorry-looking."

"Will do," Traveler replied.

Hill got to his feet and produced a map. "Excuse me, miss. Uh, just how the hell do we get out of here? I mean, we seem to be heading in a pretty raunchy direction."

"You might as well throw that map away, mister," Veronica said with a smile. "Those Glory Boys have forced you into a section of turf that is primo tough. This whole area has changed pretty drastically since the war.

"The chemical and gas explosions formed a small range of hills and valleys. The place was perking for years. Landslides. Earthquakes. The works. We now have a new little mountain range sitting between you and the desert leading straight to the border."

"Tough to get through?" Orwell asked.

"Nope. Not really. Most people go around them, though."

"That seems silly," Traveler said.

"Yeah," she admitted. "But folks here don't like those mountains much. They call them the Suicide Mountains."

"Why's that?" Hill demanded.

"Don't know," Veronica said with a shrug. "I never met anyone who got out alive to ask."

Traveler handed Hill the baby. Hill and Orwell climbed into the back of the van. "But the mountains are the fastest way?"

"Yup," Veronica said, beginning to walk toward the plane.

"Veronica?" Traveler said, trotting after her.

The young woman turned around, gazing at him inquisitively.

Traveler had just realized that he and his companions had, inadvertently, led the Glory Boys to her home. "What are you going to do when the Glory Boys get here? I mean, they'll find your dome.''

"Well," she replied, "it had to happen eventually. I don't have too much of a choice. I can't really stick around here, can I? You know what Glory Boys do to stray women. There wouldn't be enough left of me to spread on a cracker.''

She stuck a thumb upward. "It's to the skies for this flygirl.''

Traveler glanced at the Meat Wagon. "Look, there's room in the back of my van. It would be a little crowded but we could get you out of here with no sweat.''

Veronica smiled. "I appreciate your offer but this is my home. You all just watch your ass if you take the mountain route. It's pretty hairy.''

She gave him a gentle push. "Now, back off while I get this crate off the ground. You'd better beat it soon, Traveler. I figure those Glory Boys to be right over that rise behind us and gaining fast.''

"I'm out of here," Traveler said.

He backed toward the Meat Wagon as Veronica Hart cranked up the four vintage engines. She slowly taxied the plane past Traveler. "Hey," she yelled, "My father's name was Alexander Ralston Hart. Remember that, okay? I loved him.''

Traveler nodded and watched the World War II plane slowly take off into the approaching night sky. The plane buzzed the Meat Wagon once, its pilot waving one last time, before heading back into the direction from which the Wagon had just come.

Traveler sighed and walked back to the van. He started up the engine and slowly pulled away.

"Hey," Hill asked. "Where did that broad go?''

Traveler stared in the rearview mirror as the Van careened forward. "Valhalla.''

The Meat Wagon had traveled only a few minutes when the area was rocked by an explosion. Traveler glanced in the rearview mirror. A distant fireball lit up the sky. He slowed the Wagon down and watched the orange mushroom soar heavenward, clutching at the stars themselves.

"Hey," Hill said. "Let's get a move on. That broad said those Glory Boys would be here any minute.''

Traveler slipped the van into cruise control. "I have a feeling they've been detained,'' Traveler said, watching the fireball dissipate.

He glanced over his shoulder at the wide-eyed baby boy. ''Well, Alexander,'' Traveler said. ''You're certainly changing a lot of people's lives.''

''Alexander?'' Hill said, pouting. ''Who said his name was Alexander? What kind of name is Alexander?''

''Lots of great men named Alexander,'' Orwell replied matter-of-factly. ''Alexander Graham Bell. Alexander the Great. Alexander's Ragtime Band.''

Hill looked at the infant. ''Alexander the Great. Yeah. I like that.''

The Meat Wagon headed toward the border via the quickest route . . . through the Suicide Mountains.

12

The Suicide Mountains weren't mountains, exactly, but, under the baleful gaze of an emerging moon, they certainly would drive one to despair. The "mountains" were, in reality, large mounds of manmade debris mixed with untold tons of sand and grit. A terrible series of explosions must have torn the very earth asunder, causing the sand to fuse into huge walls of smooth, glistening rock.

Sections of buildings, storage tanks, and assorted trinkets of civilization had been caught in the upheaval and now protruded from this maze of upwardly spiraling walls like remnants of some discarded hallucination.

Since nearly all government installations had gardens and well-attended grounds, even the flora had been tossed into the sinister stew and now, some decade and a half after the explosion, petrified trees and flowers littered the area.

From a distance the "mountains" looked like rock hands emerging from the sand, stretching endlessly into the distance. Up close the strange formation was even more forbidding. A smooth road ran through the structure but the eerie slabs, towering some thirty or forty stories high, almost completely obliterated any traces of sky.

Staring straight down the road gave one the feeling of all-encompassing doom. It was as if the devil had paved a road through a maze once used by the Titans before their banishment from the Earth.

Traveler stopped the Meat Wagon at the beginning of the road leading through the mountains.

"Charming," he muttered. He senses were tingling. There was something awaiting all three of them in there that would pose a threat, yet the danger wasn't tangible. It wasn't something he could put into words, or even feelings. It just seemed that death was *every*where.

Orwell picked up his rifle and cradled it, peering out through the Wagon's windshield. "I don't like this," he muttered. "I don't like this at all. Reminds me of El Hiagura. Walking point in the forest. Not knowing the terrain. Not seeing anything . . . until it was too late. Then seeing too much."

Traveler couldn't argue. Anything or anybody could be hiding behind one of those dark, shining slabs of skyscraper-sized stone.

Hill left the baby in the back of the van and crawled up behind Traveler and Orwell. "Jeez," he exhaled. "Looks like a king-sized graveyard, don't it? There's nothing out there that's alive."

Traveler picked up a small pair of spyglasses and placed them to his eyes. They had infrared lenses for night tracking. Hill was right. There *was* nothing out there that even remotely appeared alive. No animals. No vegetation. Everything in front of them seemed petrified. A slice of nature caught and preserved in a death screech.

"We could go around," Traveler suggested.

"We have the Glory Boys on our butt," Orwell pointed out.

"And those funny Rasputin guys," Hill added.

The baby picked that time to emit a heart-tugging "goo." The three men looked at each other, sighing in resignation.

"Shit," Traveler hissed. "I guess that decides that."

He edged the Meat Wagon forward. Hill and Orwell both kept their heavy assault rifles ready in hand. Traveler kept his, the safety off, at his side.

After entering the mountains, they lost all contact with what was perceived as reality. All that lay before them was darkness. The headlights of the van sliced through the murk ahead. There wasn't much to see. The mountain walls stood, tilted this way and that, before them, sending the headlight beams bouncing dizzily from one side to another. It was like shining a flashlight into a house of mirrors.

Before long they noticed a thin mist clinging to the road.

Traveler thought it was odd. Mist usually meant moisture was present. He hadn't noticed any trace of water in this colossal crypt. Plus there was the fact that they were in the middle of a desert.

His thoughts were interrupted by Hill.

"Jesus H. Christ, look at that!"

Hill pointed out the side window slat at a body, or what was left of one. A skeleton in a Glory Boy uniform sat placidly on the side of the road, a corroded pistol in its hand and a large hole at the top of its skull. The skeleton's frozen grin seemed to mock the Meat Wagon and its passengers.

Its feet had been gnawed off.

"There's another one," Orwell said, gesturing to the opposite of the road.

A decomposing cadaver in a peasant's outfit was hanging from a petrified branch, which emerged from the smooth rock surface like a bony arm.

"Do you think he did that himself?" Orwell asked.

"Pretty good guess," Traveler said, nodding ahead. Three more skeletons sat by the roadside. Two had their hands around each other's throats, the other still gripped the sword it had plunged through its midsection.

Their flesh had been stripped clean.

The mist before them was growing thicker now. It was beginning to swirl up to windshield level as the car rolled onward.

Traveler's senses were afire, tingling with the presence of all-encompassing risk.

He strained his ears. He thought he heard something: high-pitched whines, followed by dull *whoomps*. He knew that sound well from his LURP days. Enemy incoming. Instinctively he crouched, remembering the first days in Latin America when, diddy-bopping through the jungle without warning, the terrain erupted with mortar fire. Somehow he had survived. In the years to come, he would learn to fire his machine gun in bursts of three. That way the enemy would never know who was carrying the M-60. The enemy had a nasty habit of trying to off the guy with the deadliest gun.

"Listen," Traveler whispered. "Hear anything?"

"And how." Orwell nodded. In the distance he could hear gruff, harsh voices coming toward the car. Mobs of insane men and women with one thing and one thing only in mind: killing.

Traveler ducked instinctively as a shell exploded nearby. That was close. He was beginning to sweat. He couldn't see the shells go off. The vast walls of glazed sand and debris hid them from view. But, from the sound of it, they were hitting damned close and getting closer.

Hill was sitting wide-eyed in the backseat. "I wish I could see the fucking sky," he muttered. "I can't see the fucking sky."

They were sitting ducks. He knew that. They were dead meat. Someone out there had choppers. He could hear them. He could hear the gunners spitting out waves of instant death. It was only a matter of time. He cradled his gun in his arms and stared up at the horrible lines of monolithic structures surrounding them.

If only he could see the fucking sky.

"Stop the car, man," Orwell yelled.

"I can't do that," Traveler shot back.

Orwell raised his rifle at Traveler's head. "Stop the fucking car, man. I want out."

"But we're in the middle of—"

Before Traveler could stop him, Orwell kicked open the passenger door and leapt out into the night. Traveler watched helplessly as the black man disappeared into the swirling mist.

"God damn it," Traveler hissed. He heard a shell explode nearby. "He's going to get killed out there."

He turned to Hill. "Wait with the kid. I'm going after Orwell."

"No way," Hill said, diving out of the car. He hit the ground and rolled into the fog, clutching his heavy assault rifle. Let them try to find him down here. He'd pepper the undersides of those choppers before they could spot him in this hellhole.

Alone in the front seat, Traveler turned and stared at the baby. "I hate to leave you alone, kid, but . . . ."

The boy child let out a terrified howl, his tiny face contorting into an anguished shape that centered around his oval mouth. The cry was so primal, so *immediate*, that it frightened Traveler. He felt the hairs on the nape of his neck slowly rise. The baby definitely did not like the idea of remaining in the car.

Traveler scooped the child up in his right arm and, cradling his rifle with his left, emerged from the van.

"Well, kid," he muttered. "You're in danger by yourself and

you're in danger with me. But I guess you'd prefer the company, eh?''

The child stopped howling. Traveler sighed and ventured into the mist. The yellowish fog seemed to take on a strange green hue. It stung Traveler's eyes. His throat burned. His lungs had trouble handling the stuff. He would have succumbed to his light-headedness had it not been for the fact that the constant barrage of shells was getting louder and louder, closer and closer. Two of his buddies were out there. As their former commander and longtime friend, he had a responsibility to bring them back to safety.

No matter what.

He grimaced and walked tentatively into the mist.

Several hundred yards in front of Traveler, Orwell staggered from monolithic wall to wall. The voices were everywhere. They were coming after him. He was afraid that this would happen one day. He had always been afraid of it coming.

He rubbed his eyes with his bearlike hand and peered into the murk. The voices were very close now. He could hear something else too. Long, plaintive bawling. Hounds. They had hounds after him!

Gradually the figures in the mist began to take shape. They were small-town men: big and burly with hands calloused from a hard day's work. Some carried torches. Others carried rifles. A squat man in the lead had three baying hounds on a tether.

The torchlight reflected off their faces in a hellish glow, illuminating the hard lines of singleminded hatred. The men paused as one. They pointed a finger at Orwell.

"There he is!" a tall fellow bellowed. "There's the nigger!"

A rounder man held up a rope. "Let's lynch him. Lynch like we did his big brother!"

Orwell turned and ran madly into the fog. The lynch mob trotted off eagerly behind him.

Down the road, Hill heard none of this. He slithered along the ground, holding his breath and clutching his rifle. The choppers were overhead now. They were thundering over the monoliths like prehistoric insects.

A searchlight reflected off the sheer slopes of the Suicide Mountains as the sleek killer copters continued their patrol. Hill flipped over onto his back, still holding his weapon tight to his chest. Just as he thought. They were Russian-made.

He held his breath as the machine-gun fire ricocheted off the ground not ten feet from where he was sprawled. Some things never seemed to change.

Traveler was entertaining similar thoughts when a shell exploded some five feet away from him. He dove for the ground, sheltering the baby, Alexander, under his chest. When the smoke and the flame cleared, he slowly got to his feet. His head was spinning. Adrenaline was pumping throughout his body, spreading a warm, tingling sensation. Every fabric of his being was alert.

He was a soldier in the middle of combat once again.

Clutching the baby in his arm, he ran into the night. Shells exploded all around him. Suddenly, out of the fog, a village appeared. It was poor and simple. Thatched huts stood on a mound of dirt. A shell erupted directly to the left of the hovels.

Traveler stopped in his tracks. The screams of children filled the air. Traveler watched helplessly as two dozen toddlers, three, four, five years of age, stumbled, dazed, from the huts. The wide-eyed children looked this way and that as the sky hissed with the shrieks of incoming artillery.

"Jesus, no," Traveler whispered. He stood, transfixed in horror, as the earth itself soared skyward, shattering both the huts and the children in one continuous *whoooomph*.

Clots of debris sailed all around him. Small red-soaked wads of human flesh flopped onto the ground before his feet. He could smell the odor of charred skin. It was sweet. Sickening. Sections of the straw roofing floated lazily down from the sky, all aflame. Some of the sections sputtered out and disappeared before reaching the earth, melting into the fog as small bursts of ashes.

Traveler didn't budge. He was numb. This was the one sight he feared most of all in battle, a sight he had seen time after time again in combat. Innocent civilians taken out by rampaging armies. Witnessing the destruction of adults was bad enough, but children . . .

Traveler shook his head sadly. It was a nightmare come alive. He looked down at the baby in his arms. The child was laughing with delight, extending a chubby hand toward one of the towering monoliths.

Traveler regarded the child with puzzlement. How could a newborn baby *not* react to the turmoil around it? Surely the kid could hear those screaming shells still falling. The baby couldn't ignore the flying debris, the disgusting smells, the horrible sights.

Traveler blinked.

Unless . . . unless there was no turmoil. No debris, no smells, no sights.

Traveler stared into the fog. Another village stood before him. No, not another village. The *same* village. A village Traveler had dreamed about for years. A village he had seen destroyed in combat nearly twenty years before.

The baby laughed out loud.

Traveler was forced to laugh as well. Somehow he was being victimized by a very realistic mirage. The kid began to cackle. The small, elfin laugh echoing in the grim surroundings made Traveler laugh even harder. His laugh was genuine, although a mixture of nervous release and spiritual exorcism. How idiotic! The damn village before him was totally Asian. In the middle of Mexico yet.

As Traveler laughed, the village before him disappeared. The shells stopped falling. The night, once again, became silent.

"God damn," Traveler whispered.

The baby burped and giggled by way of reply.

He took a closer look at the fog. He should have figured it out before this, especially since he'd been the victim of a neurotoxic gas years ago. This wasn't fog. This wasn't mist. It was the remnants of God knows what kind of gas the government once housed here. During the 1980s the U.S. was experimenting with Lord knows how many hallucinogenic gases. He and he buddies were now slogging through the Mulligan's stew of the government's efforts. A toxic dump of sorts.

He had a hunch about why he saw what he saw but he couldn't be sure until he found Hill and Orwell.

Clutching the still-gurgling child, Traveler ran back toward the car. He hoped he could find them before they fell victims to the Suicide Mountains.

Hill slithered on the ground, machine guns roaring in his ears. The choppers were overhead again, kicking up a small ocean of dust and grit. Man, this was definitely a No. 10 situation. He hadn't felt so pinned down in years.

"Hill!" came a familiar voice.

"Kiel," Hill called back into the mist. "Get down, man. This is no place to diddy-bop through."

Traveler came striding through the mist. The baby was in his right arm, laughing like crazy. Hill had to blink twice to believe the sight. The copters were careening above the twosome's heads. The bullets were zinging all around them. Yet they paid them no mind. Traveler and little Alexander seemed immune to the situation.

It was the craziest fucking thing Hill had ever seen.

He shook his head and laughed to himself. Traveler noted this and grinned back. "That's it, Hill. Laugh. It's a joke. It's all a big god-damned joke."

"What are you talking about?" Hill said.

"What are you running from?" Traveler asked.

"Those Russian choppers, man. They're all around me."

"Like they were in El Hiagura?"

"Damn straight. Just like they were in El Hiagura."

"Look at this baby, Hill. He's laughing his butt off. Do you think a kid would do that if he was being buzzed by choppers and strafed?"

Hill had to think about that. He could *see* the bullets. He could *see* the copters. He could also see the kid quite plainly. The little pixie was having a ball. Traveler was bouncing him casually against his hip. "I guess no kid would," Hill admitted. "But the choppers are all around you . . ."

"Not for twenty years. You're seeing the same choppers you saw in El Hig, Hill. I figure they're the ones you see in your dreams all the time too."

"Damn straight. I *still* have nightmares."

"You're having one now."

Hill cracked up. "No, these are real."

"Get up. Walk over here."

"You're crazy."

"Maybe. But watch this." Traveler slung his rifle over his shoulder and, placing the baby in both arms, rocked the baby to and fro while doing a stiff-legged waltz through the machine-gun fire.

"Un-fucking-believable," Hill said, beginning to giggle. "Kiel, you're out of your mind."

Hill slowly got to his feet, laughing. The more he laughed, the fewer the number of bullets zinging around him. As he walked toward Traveler, the bullets disappeared completely; so did the copters, so did the sounds of battle.

"I don't get it," Hill said.

"This mist," Traveler said. "I think it's the remnants of that chemical testing center Veronica told us about. Remember how the neurotoxin affected our nervous system? It made us sensitive to everything. I think this gas preys upon your greatest fears. I mean, this place is pretty spooky as it is, right? You're on edge just entering. A few whiffs of this shit and, before you know it, you're visualizing what your biggest nightmare is."

"And, eventually, you either go mad with fear . . ."

"Or kill yourself before someone or something else can do it for you"

"Shit."

"I guess the only way to combat it is to realize that it's just a goofy dream. Little Alexander the Great did that for me by giggling when I was watching kids getting x'd out by incoming shells. The minute I started laughing, the minute the nightmare receded."

Hill reached over and patted the baby on its tiny cheek. "Yeah. A baby wouldn't pick up on any of this crap, would it? I mean, a baby has a clean soul, right? No nightmares. No enemies. No problems."

A burst of automatic rifle fire shattered the calm. Traveler and Hill looked at each other. "Orwell," they said simultaneously. Traveler handed the baby to Hill and ran off into a cloud of the gaseous mist. "Take the kid to the van and wait."

Hill hugged the baby close and ran off in the opposite direction.

Traveler found Orwell, wild-eyed and sweating, firing off rounds at a vast wall of pulverized sand and debris. Traveler approached him cautiously.

"Orwell," he whispered. "It's me . . . it's . . ."

"Stay away from me!" Orwell screamed, pointing the rifle in Traveler's direction. Traveler hit the dirt instinctively. He had seen those slugs slice through oak trees and kill the man hiding behind them. A staccato round sizzled through the air over him and slammed into the mountain wall directly to his back. He was showered with hot, stinging shards of grit. Another round of fire dug into the ground directly next to his left leg.

"Orwell," he said, trying to keep his voice light. "You're a dummy."

"What? What? Who are you calling a dummy!"

"You. Who are you firing at?"

"I'm firing at Tibbs . . . and Sonny and Titus an—"

"Who are those guys?"

"Man. They're the townfolk. The white townfolk. They killed my brother. Donny. He was older than I was. I was a little kid. They killed him. He was marching with whites. A civil rights march."

"When was that?"

"Back in 1965."

"And they're here now? Why?"

"To get me like they got Donny."

"They must be pretty old by now, huh? I mean, they must be in their nineties, right? What are they going to do, kill you with their crutches?"

Orwell blinked for a moment. The figures of the lynch mob seemed to take a few steps backward into the mist. The townspeople glanced at each other nervously. They seemed unsure of themselves. Orwell noticed that the hounds had vanished. He now saw that Traveler was lying on the ground not twenty feet in front of him.

"Kiel, look out for the hounds!"

Traveler got to his feet, smiling. "How come there are no Mexican doctors?"

"I don't know."

"Because you can't write prescriptions with spray paint!" Traveler replied with a grin.

Orwell had to laugh. This was nuts. In the middle of a lynching, Kiel was cracking jokes. Orwell had a weakness for bad jokes. He began to laugh louder. The townspeople didn't seem to like that. The more Orwell laughed, the more frustrated the mob became. That, in turn, made Orwell laugh harder. By the time Traveler reached the man, he was roaring with laughter. By the time Traveler explained the situation, the specter of the lynch mob, long destroyed by time and nuclear war, disappeared into the night.

Hill was waiting patiently next to the Meat Wagon, baby in arms, when Orwell and Traveler emerged from the labyrinth.

"You okay?" Hill asked.

"Yeah," Orwell replied. "Freaky shit, man. Very freaky."

Hill nodded toward the kid. "Kiel said the boy here tipped him off. Pretty smart for such a short kid, huh?"

"Get in the car," Traveler said sternly.

"All right, all right," Hill muttered, climbing in the van with the child. "Why the big rush? Now that we know the secret of this place, we can cope. We're pretty safe in here for the time being."

"Think so?" Traveler said. "The mist killed those guys on the road, but something very real did the munching. I plan on being out of here before we meet the residents of this mountain range."

"No argument from me," Orwell replied, quickly climbing into the van.

Traveler sat behind the wheel and turned over the ignition. He wanted to get moving for two reasons. One, he didn't want to encounter whatever meat eaters roamed this hellhole. Two, he didn't want to lose consciousness until he was safely out in the desert.

A small pool of red formed under his left leg.

Traveler gritted his teeth and sent the van speeding forward. He sent a message to his body to shut out the pain.

His body responded as best it could. It was a difficult command to obey, however. One of Orwell's slugs had bounced off the monolith wall and torn through Traveler's left hip.

He was now losing blood.

A lot of it.

13

Three hundred men remained, poised, before the maze of monolithic structures glistening in the moonlight.

An armor-plated stretch limo purred, stationary, in the vanguard. A jeep carrying Captain Memphis pulled up alongside the limo. Memphis hopped out of the vehicle and opened the rear door of the larger car. The gnarled, twisted body of President Andrew Frayling slid out.

The embittered old man stood before the Suicide Mountains. He said nothing. Memphis watched the President work his one good eye—his right—up and down, side to side, as he took in the scope of this manmade hell.

"You're sure they went inside?" the President asked.

"As far as we can tell, sir," Memphis replied. "The tracks go directly into the structure."

Frayling stifled a laugh. "Damn fool. He's driven to his own death. Even the locals know enough not to enter that gas stove."

"Yes, sir," Memphis said without conviction.

Frayling cast a suspicious glance at his second in command. "What's the matter, Memphis? What's on your mind?"

"Well, sir, admittedly Traveler and his friends have entered the structure and, admittedly, that act alone would mean the death of most normal men . . . ."

"I hear a 'but' forming in this conversation."

"Yes, sir. But this Traveler doesn't seem to behave like most normal men."

"You're not getting as bad as these people down here, are you, Memphis? This Road Ghost bullshit. You're not trying to ascribe some supernatural powers to this—this traitorous worm!"

"No, sir. But he's a former LURP. He's very . . . resourceful."

The President was about to respond when Pope Gordon, riding a massive white stallion, charged into their midst. The robust holy man was wearing a long bearskin vest over his cassock. He resembled a postnuclear Genghis Khan. With remarkable grace for a man his size, Gordon dismounted and marched to the limousine.

"Damn his hide," Gordon blurted. "We found out what took out your advance troops."

"Took out?" the President said, confused.

"Yes, sir," Memphis injected. "We thought it best not to tell you until we had all the facts."

"That patrol you send out after Traveler got char-broiled, Scar . . . er, President Frayling."

"What!" the old man fumed, the white side of his face suddenly growing as crimson as the twisted side. "When did this happen? How?"

"Well," Gordon replied as Memphis sighed and leaned against the limo in disgust, "just a few hours ago. About five miles back. We rerouted your troops so you wouldn't march through what was left of them. Apparently it was a bomber—"

"What are you talking about?" the President demanded. "A bomber? Whose bomber?"

"It was a World War II fighter plane," Gordon continued. "It was flown suicide style into a six-by holding men and ammunition."

"What's a six-by?" the President hissed to Memphis.

"A truck, sir."

"Of course," Frayling replied. "And this six-by thing. It exploded on impact."

"That's one way of putting it," Gordon acknowledged. "From the looks of it, chunks of that truck are heading toward the planet Jupiter as we speak. It was an inferno back there, Mr. President. Only two men survived."

"Two?"

"Out of nearly a hundred."

"Have the two talked?"

"Not really."

"Why not?"

"Well, right now, sir, they're closer to the hamburger family than the human race. It's only a matter of time."

"Damn him," Frayling hissed. "Where was our intelligence on this one? Why didn't we know he had a plane at his disposal?"

"Our information didn't mention a plane, sir," Memphis said.

"Well, then our information was wrong, wasn't it?" Frayling smirked.

"It would seem so, sir," Memphis replied dully.

Frayling gazed at the mountains. "If he gets through there alive, he'll only be eight hours from the border, Memphis. Am I correct? Eight hours?"

"Yes, sir."

"Eight hours away from causing our destruction. We can't let that happen, can we, Memphis?"

"No, sir."

Frayling leaned on Gordon and lowered himself back into the limo. "All right. Then here is what we do. We split the forces in two. Gordon and I will lead our half around the mountains. If Traveler or Road Ghost or Zorro or whatever the hell he calls himself gets through that pass, we'll be waiting for him on the other side."

The President executed a half smile at Memphis. "And you, Captain, you will lead the other half of our contingent into the mountains in direct pursuit. If he has faltered in there, you will find him and eliminate him."

"Don't forget the child," Gordon cautioned.

"Of course," the President replied. "I meant, eliminate them all."

"But, sir," Memphis began, "you yourself said that those mountains are—"

The President shook his head angrily. "You are military, sir. You are above falling into obvious traps. Deal with it, Memphis. Deal with it. If you think that this mercenary can make it through those mountains working for the forces of evil, then I'm sure that you can equal his efforts, working for the forces of good."

"But—"

"You don't doubt your abilities as a soldier, do you, Memphis?'' the President asked. ''If you do, let me know now. We will relieve you of your post and give you a quick burial.''

Memphis swallowed hard. This was insanity. He realized that. But death was finality. ''If he's in there, we'll find him, sir.''

''Good,'' Frayling replied, closing the limo door.

Memphis watched silently as the limousine departed. Pope Gordon raised a large staff and yelled, ''Death to Traveler!''

''Death to Traveler!'' his monks repeated.

The Glory Boys present looked somewhat uncomfortable.

''Death to the Satan Child!'' Gordon bellowed. The monks, again, repeated his battle cry.

Gordon trotted off after the limousine. Memphis watched half his Glory Boys following suit, mixing with a large group of monks. He turned and faced the remainder of the army, two hundred troops. Monks on horseback. Glory Boys both astride horses and piled into six-bys and battered jeeps.

Memphis got into his jeep. ''Proceed,'' he told the driver.

The jeep slowly made its way into the Suicide Mountains. Memphis didn't mention the gas to anyone. Why panic the men if it wasn't necessary? If and when the men began to hallucinate, he would then turn and explain it to them. He would rely on their logic, on their reason, on their dedication to the cause to pull them through. As for Gordon's monks . . . he hoped their faith would suffice.

Memphis tensed his jaw and drew his .45 as the jeep rumbled deeper into the dark recesses of the Suicide Mountains. The world itself seemed to disappear as they rode onward into this by-product of the Third World War.

Memphis noted the skeletal remains alongside the road. He shuddered, thinking of the different horrible ways these poor assholes had died. He glanced over his shoulder. The troops were still moving forward, although their fervor seemed less intense than it had been outside the mountains.

Visibility was decreasing. A strange fog clung to the ground, enveloping the tires of the jeep. Memphis wondered what kind of denizens, either man or beast, dwelled in this area.

He could hear the men whispering behind him now. They were afraid. He'd have to level with them soon. Would they be able to comprehend what they were dealing with?

Memphis's thoughts were interrupted when the jeep came to a

screeching halt. The driver stared, mouth agape, at the ground just in front of the headlights.

"What the devil do you think—" Memphis began. He was cut short by a burst of raucous laughter. There, standing before the jeep, was a group of big, burly leather boys. Cheeks lightly rouged, eyeliner in place, and lips glossed, they stood defiantly before the jeep, their tight black leather pants revealing the extent of their interest in the jeep's contents.

Memphis swallowed hard. The leather boys were whispering to each other and grinning. They pointed, as one, toward Memphis, beckoning him forward. Calling him names he hadn't heard since that incident in the San Francisco bar. He thought he had forgotten that, put that behind him. He had been young then. Foolish. He tried to change. He had joined the service. He was a man's man now.

The leather boys ran forward toward the jeep. Memphis let out a yowl and jumped from the jeep, running deep into the fog.

His driver, meanwhile, sat petrified behind the wheel, menaced by a thirteen-foot tall facsimile of his mother.

The two hundred men behind the jeep scattered. Diving from their vehicles, they ran off the road, guns drawn. Riders spurred their horses into full gallop. The men screamed in terror, firing their guns wildly at their pursuers.

For what seemed an eternity, the imposing Suicide Mountains echoed with the cries of horrified men and the crash of panicky arms fire.

Moments later all two hundred men lay dead, destroyed by visions of ghouls, monsters, lovers, devils, warriors, teachers, nuns, preachers, driving instructors, IRS officials, immigration officers, and bankers.

Rivers of fresh blood mingled with the yellow-green fog.

A hundred riderless horses stumbled out of the mountains, faced with certain death in the desert before them.

Within the mountains, however, no vultures appeared to feed on the dead. No vulture dared to penetrate the forbidden zone to feed. This game was already spoken for.

A chorus of ghastly howls and growls soon resounded through the mazelike terrain. The citizens of the Suicide Mountains were on the prowl.

14

Traveler drove the Meat Wagon in silence, cautiously maneuvering the vehicle along the fog-enshrouded road. The mist was growing thinner now, and the headlights were able to pierce it for a distance of fifteen or twenty feet. But the road was no longer smooth. It was jagged and strewn with debris. The tires of the Meat Wagon thumped up and down over a massive skeleton picked clean. There were hundreds of skeletons lying in the road, the remnants of those who had been here before—and didn't make it. The air stung with the sound of human bones being snapped into pieces by the steel-belted radials.

Traveler couldn't be sure but he thought he sensed shadows running alongside the bone-littered road, some ten feet off the shoulder. He didn't think it was the gas. He didn't think it was the effects of the hallucinogen. He grimaced as a shard of pain made itself felt in his left hip. His entire leg was warm and sticky, coated with a drying glaze of blood.

He hoped they were getting close to the end of the mountainous road. He would be glad to get out of this graveyard. Even the unmerciful desert seemed easy to deal with at this point.

The sound of the van's motor gradually lulled the trio into a sense of controlled watchfulness. The baby napped next to Hill.

Traveler, however, couldn't shake the feeling that the van was not making this trip alone. He felt outflanked. Then he noticed it. It was imperceptible at first, a sound gradually introducing itself into the background noise of the determined Meat Wagon. Soon, however, it became a forceful component in the audio mix.

Traveler turned his head toward the back of the van. Hill and Orwell were peering out of the metal slats in the rear of the Wagon. They had noticed it too.

Was it the result of the gas? No, Traveler thought. They had intellectually defeated the toxic fumes. He noticed that little Alexander was awake as well. The tiny face was a portrait of concentration.

The noise leisurely asserted itself, growing in intensity over a period of minutes. It was a rumbling sound, distant at first; a constant, wild churning.

Orwell was the first to speak. "What do you think it is? Earthquake?"

Traveler shook his head slowly from side to side. "I'm not sure. I've never heard anything like that before."

"Maybe a flood," Orwell theorized. "I heard a flood once in Mississippi. A dam along the river broke. Sandbags wouldn't stop the water. Just slammed through this little town and flattened it. It sounded sort of like this."

"Sort of," Traveler noted. "I saw a tornado hit a trailer park in Ohio. Made one hell of a noise. Everything was quiet. Dead still. Then there was a roar. The sky opened up and this big, dark *finger* of wind just dragged itself across the land. Sucked everything up. That sounded a little like this too."

"A little," Orwell replied.

The noise rumbled louder and louder, never faltering. The baby uttered a low purr. Hill looked at the little boy. His tiny hands were curled up in fists, a cherub ready for a fight. Hill smirked and returned his gaze back to the road behind the van.

"I don't care if it's a flood or a landslide or a twister or the biggest fucking buzz saw in the history of hardware, whatever it is, it's catching up with us . . . and pretty damn fast!" Hill said.

Traveler nodded. He knew Hill was right. Placing his left hand over his torn hip, he slowly pressed down on the accelerator. The Meat Wagon began to pick up speed. Bones were flying in its wake now, as the wheels of the van spun madly over the carcasses.

Thunder boomed through the cavernous mountain range now.

Hill was the first to note the source of the rumbling. "Holy shit," he hissed. "I sure hope we're still hallucinating!"

They were difficult to discern, at first. In the wake of the Meat Wagon's dim tail lights and surrounded by fog, they seemed like only shadows, weird formations dancing up and down in the fog. But, as they grew closer, they became more distinct. It was the eyes that Hill initially noticed. They had luminescent eyes. The orbs were a sickly mixture of pale green and red and they pierced the fog with sinister glimmers.

"It's not the gas." Orwell gasped. "I've never had nightmares bad enough to imagine *that*!"

The shadowshapes burst forth from the mist, causing all three men to shiver involuntarily. The beasts bellowed and howled insanely, their roars being picked up by the towering mountains and sent echoing into space.

They were genetic freaks, more animal than human. Most of them ran semierect, like rampaging chimpanzees. Some, however, galloped on all fours, others on three limbs; two or three actually slithered forward, leaving a strange trail of slime and blood in their wake.

Their faces, such that they were, were contorted into fleshy effigies of bloodlust. Human eyes were combined with animal snouts. Large, bloodstained, almost canine fangs protruded from slashes that were meant to be mouths. Their paws were scaly and taloned. Some were covered with hair, some fur. Nonhuman ears, both rounded and pointed, twitched as they galloped, taking into account every sound the van made. Their snouts sniffed the air greedily, perhaps egged on by the soft but distinctive scent put out by Traveler's hip wound. Years of living in the tainted valley filled with the hallucinogenic vapor had totally distorted the creatures' senses. For them reality had vanished. They dwelled in a twilight realm of total insanity.

Traveler slammed on the gas. The Meat Wagon zoomed forward, sending up a thick spray of bones. The human remains bounced off the creatures' torsos with no effect whatsoever. The monsters brushed the projectiles away with a casual movement of their burly arms.

Hill and Orwell didn't speak. They merely picked up their heavy assault rifles and, placing the barrels in the slots at the rear of the van, took aim and fired. The monsters leapt forward, grasping at the van. The air crackled with the sound of gunfire.

The creatures bellowed in rage as the tiny hot lead projectiles filled the valley. The smoke given off from the rifles momentarily obscured the riflemen's view.

"Listen," Traveler whispered.

The howling had stopped. Hill and Orwell ceased firing. The smoke cleared. They pulled the guns out of the slots and peered outside into the swirling mist. The creatures were gone. The road was deserted. The only sound to be heard, once again, was the steady, frenzied hum of the van's engine and the crackling of the bones being shattered beneath its tires.

Hill and Orwell had the time to exchange one cautious glance before the van was rocked by a series of violent crashes. The top of the van bowed in slightly as Traveler fought to control the vehicle.

"Jesus!" Hill yelled. "They're diving on top of the god damn van."

Once again furious roars echoed through the mountain range.

"That's not the half of it," Traveler said with a grimace. A large claw smashed down onto the van's shatterproof windshield. Traveler didn't think twice. He grabbed his Colt .45 and fired a shot directly through the roof. A horrible creature, part lupine, part human, screeched and fell, clutching its bloodied chest. It rolled onto the hood and then in front of the van, which bobbed up in the air as it rumbled over the screeching fiend.

Traveler glanced to either side of the Meat Wagon. The mob had split into two packs. Each group was now pacing the vehicle. Traveler knew what the creatures were up to. It was a routine maneuver in both the world of animals and military minds. The two groups would keep abreast of the speeding van, eventually pulling slightly ahead. They would ever-so-slowly draw nearer and nearer to the Meat Wagon. Soon they would form a V formation in front of the vehicle, gradually squeezing the van to a stop.

Hill and Orwell caught the thought at the same time Traveler did. They looked at each other and nodded, chalking up the common revelation to either telepathy or years of experience. Without saying a word they moved to the slots on the side of the van and, sticking their heavy assault rifle barrels through the holes, opened fire on the two yammering hordes.

The animal/mutants howled and shrieked in mournful, high-pitched tones as the bullets sliced through their misshapen bodies. Much to Traveler's amazement, though, the packs never thinned. As creatures fell, mortally wounded, to the ground, other slavering beasts took their places.

Each successive wave of mutation seemed less and less human than the one preceding it. Demons that seemed to be part monkey, part ox, part jungle cat, and part reptile dove out of the mist, slashing at the careening van. Hill and Orwell didn't allow themselves the time to react to the abominations. They simply kept on firing, sending the animals skittering to the ground in explosions of blood, cartilage, mucus, and chunks of gore.

Traveler kept the van steady on the road. He was growing weak from both the mental and the physical strain. His hip was bleeding freely once again. His forehead was dotted with sweat. He couldn't keep this up much longer.

Watching the beasts continue to prowl on either side of the Meat Wagon, he was seized with a sudden rage. God damn it! He had not survived a nuclear war and then some to wind up the dinner of a group of perverted house pets. He veered the van sharply to the left and sent it hurtling into the line of carnivorous creatures. Hill continued to fire to the right of the road while Orwell clambered to the back of the van. Repositioning his gun in the rear slot, he opened fire at the confused monsters reeling in the wake of the van.

Mutation after mutation rolled over or under the speeding Wagon. Traveler gritted his teeth and began to mutter a particularly nasty version of an old pop tune. "*Something tells me it's all happening at the zoo,*" he hissed, mowing creature after creature down. "*I do believe it. I do believe it's true.*"

Orwell overheard the song and chuckled to himself. "Crazy son of a bitch," he whispered, slicing a man/bull in half with a frenzied burst of rapid fire.

"They're pulling back," Hill shouted.

Traveler glanced to the right of the road. Hill was correct. The animals had decreased their speed. They slowed to a trot before halting. Then they began to back off, allowing the van safe access through the rest of the mountain pass.

"Guess we showed those ASPCA rejects, huh?" Hill smirked.

Traveler wasn't so sure. He glanced at the stationary hordes. They weren't so much backing off from the Meat Wagon as backing away from something closing in on the auto. They were staring in the direction of the speeding vehicle but they seemed to be looking beyond it. They seemed to be looking at something . . .

. . . else.

Traveler quickly snapped his attention to the middle of the road. He just had time to realize that the road wasn't there when the Meat Wagon was lifted up into the air and the headlights focused on the biggest pair of pectorals seen since King Kong went into retirement.

"What the fuck?" Hill yelled, tumbling toward the back of the van.

The baby slid along the floor, coming to a rest at Orwell's feet. Orwell dropped his gun and swooped the baby up into his arms as the van was dropped back down onto the road and, apparently, kicked. The sputtering vehicle slid, sideways, into a monolith.

Traveler grimaced in pain as the jolt opened the gash in his hip wider. The van slapped flat against the monolith, apparently undamaged. Traveler glanced out the driver's window and saw the cause of their sudden change of direction.

There, in the middle of the road, was a creature like no other he had ever seen in fact or fantasy. It stood some ten feet high. Its torso was human as were its arms. Its legs were scaled yet its feet were cloven. Its face . . . its face was somewhat oxlike, a hideous mixture of man and monster.

A steady stream of foam dribbled from its malformed mouth.

Traveler wondered just what combination of genes, radiation, and animal formed this freak of nature. He also wondered just how long it would take before the creature decided to kick the van again and stomp its human inhabitants into something resembling Cheez Whiz.

The creature stood in the middle of the road and bellowed.

Traveler glanced in the back of the van. Orwell and Hill were dazed. The baby stared directly at Traveler. "Don't worry, kid," Traveler said. "I've gotten out of worse."

That wasn't exactly true.

Traveler kicked the driver's door opened. Blood was running freely from his wound now. His left leg was stiff. His head was light. Every muscle in his body was on fire. He grabbed his heavy assault rifle and slid out of the van, struggling to stay on his feet.

He glanced behind him. One hundred yards away, a few hundred of the creatures watched silently as the leader of their pack pawed the ground with its hoofs.

Traveler staggered toward the giant, his vision blurred, his senses swimming.

The monster snarled as the puny mortal approached. It lifted its head and roared in defiance. It twisted its scarred hands into fists and beat its massive chest in a show of power. It stomped the earth with its powerful hoofs, causing a small ground tremor.

Traveler staggered to within twenty feet of the immense beast.

The creature lowered its head and bellowed at the minuscule man. It readied itself for a charge. It shook its shoulders, beat its chest, scraped the ground, and twisted its mouth into a savage grin.

Traveler sighed, raised his rifle, and shot the monster's balls off.

The surprised giant stared at the gaping hole in its groin incredulously. It flashed Traveler one last puzzled look before collapsing to the ground in a heap.

Traveler heard a stampede behind him. He turned around. The road was empty. The creatures were gone.

"The king is dead," he muttered. "Long live modern technology."

Traveler hurried back to the van. He tossed the rifle into the front seat, positioned himself behind the wheel of the Meat Wagon, shifted the van into drive, and then passed out cold.

15

He awoke in darkness. He was shivering. His body was caught, alternately, in blinding flashes of heat and cold. His gaze was focused straight ahead. There were stars appearing in the slowly deepening blue sky.

"How are you feeling?" he heard Orwell ask.

He blinked through the sweat. "I've felt better."

"I took out the bullet," Orwell replied with a look of concern, "cauterized the wound, and covered you with a healthy dose of tequila."

"What a waste of liquor," Hill cracked, slowly coming into focus.

"How much time have we lost?" Traveler asked.

"You were out for a while," Orwell replied. "We've lost about a day."

Traveler cursed himself for being so weak. He should have been able to take it. He had been trained to take it. When still a teenager he had been plucked from suburbia and tossed into the U.S. Armed Forces. Plucked from video arcades and high-school lecture halls and plunged headfirst into war, machinery, killing, and gore, he had hardened, toughened. Why did he have to weaken now?

He knew. He was exhausted. Mentally. Physically. Spiritually.

He struggled to sit up. "We have to get going."

"Not just yet, my friend." Orwell frowned. "We have a little bit of a problem."

"You're kidding me," Traveler said, sinking down on his elbows. "Imagine us having a problem."

"It's the baby," Orwell began.

"What's the matter with the baby? Was he hit?"

"No," Hill answered. "It's nothin' like that. We were getting it together right about the time you were passing out. We drove out of that roller-coaster ride pretty damn quick. The creatures never came back after you turned their leader into a choirboy. We got out without a scratch. All of us."

"Where are we now?" Traveler asked.

"Just on the other side of the range," Orwell answered.

"The baby is *sick*, Kiel," Hill blurted. "Real sick."

"What's the matter with him?" Traveler replied.

"We don't exactly know," Hill said, his voice sounding as if it was ready to tip headfirst into panic. "His breathing is short. Shallow. Labored, sort of. His lungs sound all wheezy. His nose, Kiel. It's just caked with snot. His eyes are filled with fluid. He's feverish."

Traveler pulled himself painfully to his feet. He staggered to the van and looked inside. The baby's pale face was ablaze. His tiny chest heaved up and down in a spasmodic rhythm as he struggled to breathe. Little Alexander's mouth emitted a harsh, croupy groan with each breath. Traveler extended a hand and placed it gingerly on the child's forehead. The baby was burning alive with fever.

Traveler was both concerned and enraged. He had not taken this kid all this way for the little bastard to die because of some idiotic flu bug.

Traveler spun around and faced his two friends. "What about antibiotics? Do you have any in the fridge? I used to carry a whole emergency kit in there."

"We have antibiotics, all right," Orwell answered, walking forward and easing Traveler onto a log next to the van. "But the problem is, my man, that you are not in too fine shape yourself. You're running a temperature. You're weak from loss of blood and your wound is infected. You could use a large dose of the antibiotics yourself."

"Yeah." Hill nodded. "But the rub is . . . there's not enough of the stuff to go around."

Traveler didn't have to think about it. "Give it to the kid."

"We wanted to ask you first," Orwell said.

"You shouldn't have waited for me," Traveler said. "The baby might have taken a turn for the worse. I'll survive."

"You're in a bad way, Kiel," Orwell reemphasized.

"The kid gets the antibiotics."

Hill leapt to his feet and scurried toward the van. "I told you he'd say that." He beamed at Orwell.

Hill climbed inside the van and prepared to give the baby a shot of tetracycline.

Traveler and Orwell remained outside. Traveler tried to focus his eyes. There seemed to be two Orwells in front of him.

Orwell smiled thinly. "You might not make this one, Kiel," he said as calmly as possible. "We're in the middle of nowhere. I don't know how far we have to go before we hit the border and somewhere out there are bound to be more Glory Boys and Lord knows what else who will try to stop us from reaching the States. You're in no condition to travel, let alone fight. I can't begin to figure how much blood you lost, and your hip . . . your hip wound just won't close."

"Don't sweat it." Traveler coughed. "You may have to do the driving, that's all. I can still hold a gun and if I can't exactly see where I'm firing it, I can still *sense* where I'm shooting."

Orwell laughed softly. "Yeah, you and your voodoo sixth sense. You probably could survive a firefight totally blind. I just wanted to level with you, that's all. I respect you, man. We're brothers, you know? We've been through it all."

Traveler nodded. He was glad he was wearing a headband. Without it, he was sure that his skull would burst. "Yeah. I know."

He shrugged. "But what's the worst thing that can happen to me? I'll die. Okay. Maybe it's not as bad as people think it is. I mean, I'll die fighting, I suppose. Or maybe I'll die in my sleep. At least I won't wind up being anyone's dinner."

He flashed a feverish grin at the worried Orwell. "Who knows? Maybe the kid in there will take my place one day, just like my own kid would have. Traveler Junior."

He shook his head back and forth, his vision growing more and more blurred. "Nah. That doesn't sound right. Traveler II. That's better. Who'd ever be scared of a mercenary named 'junior'?"

Orwell leaned forward. He spoke distinctly, trying to penetrate

Traveler's mental haze with his words. "We're going to have to move out soon, Kiel. Under the cover of night. The way I figure it, whoever is on our ass wouldn't be stupid enough to send all their men into those mountains after us.

"That means whoever is left is either circling the range right now or waiting somewhere ahead of us. Nearby. We can't stay here any longer."

Traveler nodded affirmatively. He lurched to standing position. "You're absolutely right."

Hill returned from the van. He gave Traveler a concerned look. Traveler ignored it.

"How's the kid?" Traveler asked.

"He's sleeping. I gave him a good shot of that stuff."

"Good. Good," Traveler muttered, swaying dangerously. "You take care of him, okay?"

"Will do," Hill said solemnly.

"Okay," Traveler said. "Let's hit the road. We have a lot of turf to cover."

He careened toward the Meat Wagon, coming to an unsteady halt next to the driver's door. He opened the door and leaned inside. The steering wheel loomed before him eerily, glowing like one of the rings of Saturn. The dashboard undulated like an ocean wave. He pulled his head out of the car, turning to Orwell.

"You drive," he said.

"Whatever you say," Orwell said.

Hill took Traveler by the elbow and carefully maneuvered him to the back of the van. He lifted him gently and placed him inside, then climbed in after him. Traveler sat crosslegged and leaned against the side of the van as Orwell hit the ignition. He felt his consciousness ebb as the Meat Wagon pulled away.

"Hey, Kiel," Hill said. "*Kiel*. Why don't you tell me about how you looked for us for all those years after the big nuke-out? About how you just *sensed* we were still alive."

Traveler nodded and smiled. He hadn't heard exactly what Hill had asked but he knew the underlying meaning. Hang on to consciousness, man. Keep talking. Keep your mind active. Don't fall asleep again. Stay awake.

Or die.

16

The Meat Wagon plunged through the desert night with desperate speed. Orwell, at the wheel, had no idea where he was or where he was going. The compass strapped haphazardly on the dashboard read "north," and that seemed good enough. Somewhere, out beyond the headlights of the van, was the United States and, hopefully, safety.

He kept one eye on the road and one eye on the dashboard where the Geiger counter plinked lazily, indicating that the radiation in the area was well below the hazardous level.

In the back of the van, the baby slept.

Hill kept a watchful eye on Traveler, who lapsed in and out of fever delirium. Traveler fought to keep himself awake, fought to keep himself sane. Somewhere along the route, he had lost command of time. Everything was present tense. He was a teenager, a soldier, a husband, a father, a postnuclear mercenary, and a dying man all at once. He vaguely knew what was happening but, regarding it with a detached calmness only known to the dead and the dying, he didn't find it particularly interesting.

He forced his eyes open and gazed upon the innocent child lying not three feet to his right.

He didn't mind dying if it meant the baby would live. It gave him a sense of purpose.

Without warning, his head snapped back. His eyes dilated. His mind spiraled into sharp focus.

"Stop the van," he commanded.

His voice sounded so sure, so in control that Orwell, forgetting Traveler's weakened condition, instinctively brought the Meat Wagon to a fishtailing halt in the middle of the desert.

"Are you okay?" Hill asked.

Traveler wasn't but his intuition was. "They're out there," he announced. "Waiting for us."

Hill and Orwell exchanged dubious glances. Traveler caught the looks. "Don't ask me how I know, I just do," he said, bristling.

Orwell cut the headlights and stared out into the desert. The vast expanse of land before him was lit by the white light of the heavens. It was empty. Deserted.

"I can't see anything but sand," Orwell stated.

Traveler was scrambling to his feet. "They're not stupid, Orwell," he said, fighting dizziness. "They haven't survived this long by standing in front of their prey yelling 'Here we come, ready or not.' "

He picked up his crossbow, his heavy assault rifle, and checked the Ninja stars under his wristband. "I'm walking point. You follow. Keep fifty or sixty yards behind me. Keep the headlights off. First sign of trouble, take the kid and head north. I'll try to catch up. No matter what, get him safely into the States and let Jefferson know about the pope, his army, and the renegade Glory Boys. Trust your instincts and don't look back."

Traveler reached into the front section of the van and removed the satchel he had prepared in the town a few days before. It was filled with nail grenades and pipe bombs.

"Kiel, are you sure you're strong enough?" Orwell asked.

Traveler didn't answer. He grabbed the sack, jumped out of the back of the Meat Wagon, and began walking slowly into the desert.

His head ached. His hip wound throbbed. The cold desert wind evaporated the beads of sweat covering his body on contact, sending him into a constant wave of quivering. He felt almost as deranged as he had, years ago, when first hit by the neurotoxin. Every sense seemed heightened. Everything was ultra.

He saw nothing suspicious before him.

The desert was lifeless. Bleak. An endless stretch of dead white lying under a sparkling night sky.

Traveler continued to plod onward, feeling like a flea traipsing across a cadaver.

His senses were afire. There was danger out there. He felt it. But where? Nothing seemed amiss. Perhaps he was wrong. Perhaps he was hallucinating. It was the fever. The exhaustion. The infection.

He stopped suddenly. His body stiffened. He ran his right hand through his close-cropped, matted hair. No. He wasn't wrong. Something was about to . . .

A flicker of movement in the starlit dunes caught his eye. He spun around. The desert erupted. Sand-covered canvas flaps shielding well-dug trenches were flipped back, and Traveler found himself facing rows of Glory Boys and black-cowled monks.

His perception altered by the fever, Traveler watched the scene unfold in slow motion. His body screamed in pain as he spun from his left to his right, watching more and more sections of the desert erupt, revealing heavily armed men.

The rifles in their hands fired. The staccato bursts crackled in Traveler's ears like splintering timber. Traveler saw the brilliant orange flashes spit from the gun barrels. He heard the bullets whiz by him. He felt the heat. Urging his sagging muscles into action, he whirled and faced the Meat Wagon.

"Go!" he bellowed, his voice sounding like a thunderstorm in his brain. "Go!"

A flare exploded high in the air.

Its angry white and orange light blinded Traveler, sending his equilibrium into a tailspin. He collapsed on the ground in a heap, his only consolation the sound of the Meat Wagon revving its engines and hurtling off into the night.

The flare faded and died.

Traveler felt the air above him sizzle with the constant hum of rapid fire. Without thinking, he wrapped his left hand around a pipe bomb, lit it, and hurled it blindly in front of him.

He flopped over on his side to watch the results. With a tremendous *ka-thump*, the desert before him regurgitated a half-dozen screaming men with a horrible flash of red and yellow.

A strange madness enveloped Traveler. In rapid succession he lit and threw a half-dozen pipe bombs into the night. *Ka-thump*. *Ka-thump*. Blood and thunder. Screams and sand. He squirmed into a standing position and, placing his heavy assault rifle before him, charged wildly in the general direction of the trenches ahead, firing madly, with total abandon.

The enemy returned the fire but, miraculously, did not get a bead on the charging lunatic. Traveler continued to run crazily toward the ambushers, the gun pumping back and forth in his hand as he squeezed off round after round. His brain was on fire. The gun belched out flame and smoke. The night seemed alive with deadly energy.

Traveler stumbled into a trench. Two dozen men were sprawled within, maimed and moaning. Many of them were already dead. All of them would be soon.

Traveler stuck his head above the trench. He ducked back down quickly as a flurry of tracer bullets lit the sky around him. They knew he was inside their line. They were determined to kill him.

Well, Traveler thought with a shrug, fuck them.

He calmly took a nail grenade from the sack around his waist and crawled out of the trench. He slithered along the sand, the sound of automatic fire echoing through his fevered brain. Coming within twenty feet of the next trench, he lit the grenade, using his body as a shield to block the flame from the sight of the enemy, and calmly tossed it in front of him.

He then covered his head as the grenade rolled into the trench. He heard the men scream as the explosive detonated, sending thousands of tiny but lethal bits of metal slicing through their bodies.

Traveler heard the small scraps of human flesh land around him after the explosion. They hit the sand so rapidly that it reminded him of the sound of rain pelting down against a lawn on a hot summer night.

Traveler continued his murderous route forward. He leapt into the bombed-out trench. More tracers sizzled above him. He kept low. For every tracer bullet you saw, there were probably four to six regular rounds keeping it company.

He didn't pay attention to the fragged and moaning monks in the trench. He stepped over one wide-eyed boy in a cowl. The boy was making a conscientious effort to hold his intestines inside his ruptured stomach.

Traveler found what he was looking for: an 80 Mike Mike, an 80-mm mortar. There were a couple of shells left. Traveler swung the weapon around and pointed it, haphazardly, at whatever was to the rear of the trench. He fired off the two rounds and then dove out of the trench before the enemy could fire back.

Traveler had crawled about thirty yards from the trench before it was blown to bits. At least the young monk wouldn't have to worry about his roving intestines anymore.

There was pandemonium all around him. Glory Boys and monks were barking orders at one another. One man behind enemy lines could make a big difference when it came to strategy.

Conventional warfare tactics went out the window when faced with guerrilla fighting.

Traveler smirked to himself. It was a lesson most American military personnel learned all too late.

Bullets were ricocheting everywhere. The ambushers were firing at anything that moved. As a result, they were often shooting at each other. Traveler kept his head low and continued crawling forward.

He didn't fire much now. He had no need to. The ambushers were slowly destroying themselves.

Sulphur-tinged smoke, caused by both the guns and the explosives, clung to the sand. Traveler could hardly see. He was dripping wet, the fever sending his body into overdrive. His mind was fuzzy and his hands were shaking. Every so often he would wink out of the desert encounter and flip into jungle combat mode. At times he didn't know who the enemy was: El Hiaguran rebels, roadrats, mutants, Glory Boys . . .

It didn't matter.

He saw a deserted trench some ten feet ahead. He crawled forward, the sky exploding above him. He dove into the trench, hitting the bottom with a resounding thump, then scrambled to his feet.

Ten Glory Boys, rifles in hand, stared at Traveler in shock. "What the hell are you doing in here?" one of them wondered out loud.

Good question.

Traveler froze, a sickly grin on his face. "Hell of a night, isn't it?"

The Glory Boys raised their rifles toward Traveler. Traveler stood, motionless. There was nothing he could do. He shrugged. Oh, well, at least he had caused them some trouble.

He held that thought as the ground below his feet gave way. A searing flash of white light turned the Glory Boys before him into negative images. Instant still photos. Traveler's senses reeled as a thunderclap pinned his brain to the back of his head. He actually saw stars. Just like in a cartoon.

Incoming.

Mortar.

Direct hit.

The most ludicrous aspect of it all was that it was friendly fire. These Glory Boys had just been taken out by a round fired from their own buddies. Traveler would have laughed if he could have figured out how to make his mouth work . . . or even figure out which end of his body his mouth was located on. His senses spun like a carousel with major gears loose.

He fell back onto something semisolid. He slid down along something wet and warm. His mind attempted to free itself from his tumbling body. He was concussed. He was still sliding.

After an eternity, he hit bottom. Things seemed to be slipping all over him. Snails leaving slime trails. He was alternately floating and pinned down by an oppressive weight.

He located the muscles controlling his eyes and forced his lids to flutter. Finally he coaxed them to open. He was staring at the sky. He tried to turn his head. He was wedged in by something. He shifted his gaze as much as he could. He was sprawled across pieces of the Glory Boys' bodies. He was staring face to face with the top half of a kid half his age.

He felt his muscles contract suddenly. The Pucker Factor. He couldn't hear a thing. Bullets were still flying above him but he couldn't hear them. He could see them but now they were making no noise whatsoever.

He was afraid to try to move his body. If he couldn't, it would probably mean that he was dead. He didn't have the strength to move his head forward so he couldn't actually see if he was still in one piece. He commanded his fingers to wiggle. Yeah. They seemed all there. Next, a harder trick. His toes. Try to wiggle the toes. Traveler felt his toes slap against the bottom of his boot. All present and accounted for.

But wait. He had been in combat long enough to know that guys who had had their legs or arms blown off often felt pain in

their limbs long after they were gone. Phantom pains. For all
Traveler knew, he was a head with no body.

With a superhuman effort, he shook his head free of the human
debris around him. He placed his chin on his chest. His body was
still there. He stared at it carefully. It didn't look like anything
was broken. His arms and legs were splayed in natural angles. As
he took mental inventory of his bodily parts, the sound to the
picture slowly began to rise. The *pop, pop, popping* of automatic
weapons once again rang out.

Traveler attempted to wrest himself free of the scrambled
corpses but decided against it. Let the enemy think he was dead
or, better yet, let them think he had escaped. He could extricate
himself later.

He tried to relax as the sound of the firing receded into the
background. He closed his eyes. He dozed.

He was awakened by the toe of a boot digging into his left
side. He winced.

He stared up at the imposing figure of Pope Gordon. "I told
you he wasn't dead." The robed man sneered. "It's an old merc
trick, playing possum. He's not dead . . . but he's going to wish
he was real soon."

Two robed men reached down and yanked Traveler to his feet.
Someone relieved him of his rifle. Someone else ripped the
crossbow from his back.

"A pleasure to meet you, Lieutenant Paxton," came a feeble
voice from the haze before him. Traveler blinked his eyes and,
slowly, focused his gaze on the gaunt man in the walker.

Traveler tried to control his surprise. There, before him, stood
the rotting body of President Andrew Frayling. The President
half smiled, his grin disappearing under the charred section of his
face.

The President dragged himself to within inches of the beleaguered
mercenary. "This is the first time we've met . . . face to face."
He fingered the burns running from his scalp to his shoulder.
"Such that it is."

Frayling clutched his walker until his knuckles were white.
"You and I have quite a history, Lieutenant Paxton. We have
quite a lot to catch up on."

A jeep rumbled up to the trench. The President smiled lovingly at his feverish prey. He then turned to Gordon. "Strip him. Tie him. Toss him in the back."

The President watched as Traveler was dragged off by two robed thugs. He began whistling to himself. It was a tune he had loved since childhood: "Give Me That Old Time Religion."

Pope Gordon was not as festive. "The baby got away."

"Don't fret, Mr. Peissler, I'm sure we can convince our guest that it would be in his best interest to cooperate with us in locating your little messiah."

"How can you be sure?"

The President cackled into the cold desert air. "Oh, Mr. Peissler. I'm probably the most knowledgeable expert on torture alive today."

Gordon was puzzled. "Really? You saw a lot of combat? World War II? Korea? Nam?"

The President shook his head ruefully. "No. No. No. Better than that."

"Better?"

"I starred in over eighteen war films, Peissler. Over eighteen. We had some of the most creative minds in Hollywood dreaming up new and excitingly visual ways to humiliate and degrade prisoners of war."

The President pursed what was left of his lips into a disdainful pucker. "We made real warfare look like situation comedy." Then he gripped his walker and waddled off to his awaiting limo.

A sadistic smile played across Gordon's face as he watched the bloodthirsty cripple climb into the long black limousine. This was going to be good.

He loved show business.

17

The Meat Wagon sped through the sand-strewn wasteland. Orwell clutched the wheel, his face frozen, expressionless. Only the fluctuations of his jaw muscles beneath his smooth black skin betrayed the fact that he was tense. He was slowly, methodically, grinding his teeth together, up and down, back and forth.

In the back of the van, Hill sat morosely. The baby was cradled in his arm. The baby didn't cry. He didn't gurgle. He didn't make a sound. He merely stared solemnly into the haggard face of his benefactor.

Neither Hill nor Orwell had spoken for hours. Finally Hill broke the silence.

"Do you think he'll catch up with us?"

Orwell stared at the bleak landscape ahead. "If anyone can, it's Kiel."

"Then maybe we should slow down?"

"I don't think so."

Silence.

Hill gazed at the baby. "Do you think we should go back for him?"

"If we didn't have the baby to take care of," Orwell said with a sigh, "I wouldn't think twice about it. But our whole mission is tied up in this kid, right? I mean, that's why we've taken all the chances we have. This kid was important to Kiel."

Orwell frowned. He was referring to his buddy in the past tense already. Not optimistic. Maybe just realistic. "*Is* important to Kiel. He wants the kid delivered stateside safely. If we go back, there's a good chance we won't be able to get out a second time. We can't risk it for the kid's sake.''

Hill nodded slowly. ''You're right.''

''Yeah''—Orwell nodded—''but that doesn't make me feel any better.''

''Me neither.''

Orwell stared vacantly into the distance. ''Jesus, will you take a look at that!''

A herd of *something* was slowly moving toward the van. They looked a little like horses only they were . . . *different*. They trotted along on all fours. Their bodies were, roughly, horse-shaped but the skin was covered with sores and boils. They were vaguely hairy and the lower portions of their legs were stocky and cumbersome.

Orwell instinctively slowed the Meat Wagon down. Hill placed the baby in a makeshift bed he had constructed out of blankets and tin cans and picked up a heavy automatic rifle. ''What the hell are they?''

''Looks like a product of mutation and inbreeding,'' Orwell noted.

''You think it's a trap?''

''Can't be sure.''

Hill slid up into the empty space next to the weapons rack to Orwell's right. ''Keep it slow. Remember how the El Hiagurans used to use buffaloes as a shield? The little suckers would sidle up to a couple of 'em and squat down real low in the tall grass. A couple of government soldiers would walk by, see only the buffalo, and diddy-bop by.''

Orwell nodded. ''Diddy-bop straight to kingdom come.''

Hill strained his eyes for any glimpses of human forms mixed within the freakish animal herd. ''You got it. Man, I remember watchin' movies when I was a kid with cowboys and Indians and stuff. Those Indians, man. They'd run through buffalo herds and deers and stuff. They'd wear a pelt on their back so the cowboys wouldn't notice—''

''Yeah,'' Orwell interrupted, ''I catch your drift, Hill.''

The gaggle of weary beasts gazed around the desert terrain nervously. Orwell didn't like that. They looked confused, disoriented. Something had driven them from their natural habitat.

Something unexpected. Something frightening. They didn't belong in this harsh desert heat any more than Orwell, Hill, and the child did.

The animals came to a dead stop as soon as they spotted the Wagon.

Orwell shifted the van into park and waited for something to happen. There could be an ambush in the offing. A little caution now could pay off later. For a few moments neither the animals nor the vehicle made a move. The two types of beasts regarded each other with suspicion. The humans suspected the animals of being a trap. The animals, not knowing what means of destruction this metallic slug represented, hung back.

"What are we going to do?" Hill whispered. "They're just standing there."

"We're going to wait," Orwell answered. "If there *are* roadrats or worse in that herd, let them come to us."

The minutes dragged on. Finally what passed for the leader of the herd made a few hesitant steps forward. The rest of the herd fanned out behind him; a natural, instinctive move. The leader paused. The Wagon made no threatening gestures. The animal hobbled forward a few more steps. Still no reaction from the van. The animal, feeling quite confident now, increased its pace to a trot. The herd did likewise.

The leader of the herd was about three hundred feet from the van when it suddenly blew up, simply exploded.

Orwell watched, dumbfounded, as the animal went from discernible shape to a flash of fire and smoke and large wads of shattered matter.

"What the—" was all he had time to say before the herd scattered. Half were able to retreat.

The other half was pulverized in deafening roars and blinding streaks of white, searing light.

Orwell began gritting his teeth in earnest. The screams of the fleeing animals triggered memories of similar cries made by frightened humans years ago.

Foot soldiers in motion. Some tumbling forward. Some falling back. Some blowing straight up. Some were victims of frag bombs. Others were marked as sweethearts of Bouncing Bettys. Bouncing Bettys were bad news. Land mines of the worst kind. In the middle of the jungle, your foot would hit a spring beneath you and old Bouncing Betty, she'd sail up from somewhere else. The little baby would just pop right up in the air, leap four or five feet, and then . . . good night, mother.

When she'd blow, she'd spray down and she'd spray out. The only thing you could do was hit the ground fast and hard. Just hold on to the earth and pray for some quirk of absurdism to save your ass. If you were the closest to the thing, there was a slim chance that you'd get by. The fragments usually sprayed outward pretty fast. Those closest and lowest sometimes got away with just a few hunks of metal and some time in the hospital. As for the rest . . .

The scary thing about Bouncing Bettys was that, no matter how careful you were, there was always the chance that some asshole nearby would hit one and that old Betty would come leaping up right in front of you. Just like one of those cartoon characters from way back when. Like Daffy Duck or someone. They'd bounce up right in front of you. Wooo wooo wooo.

Guerrilla fighters had come up with a variety of deadly impact bombs. It was an art, really. An exercise in creative survival. Bombs in old C-ration cans. Bombs triggered off by tree limbs swinging, rocks rolling, a little pressure here, a little pressure there.

Orwell held his breath as the horse creatures skittered across the desert, getting torn apart as they galloped.

After a few moments, it was all over. The desert directly in front of them was littered with bone and fleshy debris. The horses that were able to get away had. Maybe a half dozen of them galloped madly away from the scene.

Hill and Orwell sat motionless in the front seat of the Meat Wagon. They glanced nervously at the sand stretching out on either side of the van, not knowing quite what to do.

They both realized they were in very deep shit at the moment.

They had blithely driven into a minefield.

Now they had to attempt to drive back out.

18

Traveler awoke in darkness. A blindfold had been tied around his eyes. He was kneeling . . . after a fashion. Propped up on his knees, his wrists had been pulled back behind him. Each wrist had been tied to an ankle. As a result, Traveler was kneeling with his forehead tipped toward the ground. The easiest reaction, of course, would have been to simply fall forward or sideways and rest. Something inside him, however, told him he shouldn't.

Blackness was all he saw. His hearing, however, was unimpaired. He could hear the rumble of trucks and jeeps, the clomping of horses' hoofs. A walkie-talkie squealed from somewhere nearby. He was surrounded by men, probably hundreds of them. Gordon and Frayling were planning some sort of major move, some last-ditch effort to make a point.

It all seemed so ludicrous. All these men and all this weaponry summoned up to wipe out two fleeing veterans and a bastard child.

A sudden chill swept over his body. He almost tumbled forward. He caught himself in time, however, and reared his torso back as far as he could. The movement was quick and spasmodic, like a young colt's when reacting to a hastily yanked rein.

"Excellent," a soft voice announced from nearby. "Your reflexes are amazing, considering . . ."

Traveler recognized the voice of President Andrew Frayling. It was gentle and even. The voice of anyone's "kindly old grandfather." The kind of voice that could convince you that the speaker cared. The kind of voice that offered friendship. The kind of voice that inspired leadership. The kind of voice that could lead a nation into the most illogical war in history . . . and did.

Traveler addressed the air before him. "Is this blindfold necessary?"

"For the moment," Frayling replied. "Indulge me in a bit of melodrama, Lieutenant Paxton. After all, I have allowed you to pursue your clichéd brand of heroism for several years now, have I not?"

Traveler smirked. A scream of pain rumbled around his hip.

"You seem to be the worse for wear at the moment," Frayling continued. "You're feverish. Your hip is infected. You're probably even suffering from dehydration. My goodness, if something isn't done soon I'm afraid you will be nothing more than a Road Ghost. I have a doctor standing by, you know. A very good man, not at all a hack like most of the practicing physicians in this god-forsaken area.

"I've had Dr. Mead by my side since before the war. I can guarantee you that he'll have you feeling much better in a matter of hours."

The voice sounded *so* sincere, *so* concerned, that Traveler almost found himself wavering. He shook his head clear of such thoughts and nearly fell over. He quickly righted himself. "I never knew you to be that altruistic, Frayling," he said evenly.

"Well," the voice replied with a slight chuckle, "actually, I was hoping we would make an exchange. Your good health for just a teensy bit of information."

"Like where my friends are?"

"That would be nice, yes," Frayling replied, "although, I must confess, I don't give a tinker's damn about your friends."

Frayling was lying. Traveler realized that. The President was marching toward the border and it wasn't for his health. Frayling, however, padded the ruse even further. "Yes, indeed," he continued. "I have nothing against your friends . . . or against you, for that matter. Let bygones be bygones is my feeling about things. Oh, I know I bluster sometimes and mutter things about revenge and the like but, deep down inside, I'm a good man, a Christian man. I turn the other cheek as much as possible. And when I can't do that, I turn the other scar. Aheh heh heh heh."

The President's voice rasped like a buzz saw slicing through soft wood.

"Admirable quality," Traveler managed to reply. His head was beginning to throb. His legs wouldn't hold out much longer.

"If I *did* manage to locate your two friends, do you know what I'd be inclined to do?"

"I give up."

"I'd probably just let them go. Yes, indeed. That's probably exactly what I'd do. You see, this whole search party is really Peissler's idea. You know, that fellow who thinks he's a pope? Well, he has this, this *thing* about that baby you people abducted. I don't know. Maybe he's its father or something. But, for whatever reason, he wants that child. Now, Gordon's an ally of mine so, I figure, what's the harm in helping? After all, I need all the allies I can get at this point, right? If there's anyone in the world who understands the fragility of my current position, it's you, Lieutenant. Aheh heh heh. After all, you put me here almost singlehandedly.

"I am a man without a country, for the time being. Pitiful, eh? I need a place to hide, a place to heal. Gordon can be my benefactor in Latin America.

"So, now that you can empathize with my situation and comprehend the beneficial treatment which awaits you after you cooperate, I'm sure that good judgment will prevail—"

"Eat shit."

The President's voice halted abruptly. Traveler felt as if he had just slammed his fist into the ancient madman's midsection, momentarily knocking the wind out of him. The voice promptly recovered its equilibrium.

"I trust that was merely a Pavlovian exercise in advance macho, Lieutenant. It doesn't reflect your years in the field. Now, as for the whereabouts of the child."

"What does Peissler want to do with the baby when he finds it?" Traveler asked.

"Well, er, I assume he wants to kill it. It's a religiously based paranoia but, actually, there doesn't seem to be much harm in it. The way I see it, Peissler would be doing the babe a favor, don't you think? Survival in this world is such a damned unfortunate affair. A child doesn't have much of a chance. Not at all the way it was in my day."

"I bet."

"Well," the President said, sighing. "What do you say?"

"Eat shit."

The President's voice was slowly becoming more brittle. His breathing was growing rapid and short. He was losing it. Traveler was loving it. Frayling tried to be firm but diplomatic.

"Let me tell you a story, Lieutenant. It's a story about a soldier I knew, a very brave man. In some ways you remind me of him. His name was Philip Albertine. We grew up together. We were both California kids. Zany. Athletic. Upper middle class. We had everything we could want, really.

"We were the best of pals. I became an actor. Philip joined the army. He became one of the Second World War's most highly decorated soldiers. Everyone was impressed. I envied him. He was a real hero. He, in turn, envied me. I knew Zsa Zsa Gabor personally. Once I even saw Marilyn Monroe in her underwear. Life was good.

"When my film career lagged, I went into television. I hosted *Wild West Theater* for years. I became a commercial spokesman for nuclear energy. Philip entered politics. He ran for the Senate and made it. He was one of California's best and brightest.

"And it came to pass that I, too, pondered running for office. Television increased my popularity immeasurably. My speaking for the nuclear industry opened certain political doors for me. I decided to run for governor of the state. And, irony of ironies, there was only one other person who seemed like a strong contender for the same position. Any guess who?"

"Bigfoot?"

"Philip Albertine. My old, loyal friend. My staunchest childhood ally. He was the only person who stood between me and the governorship. Well, you could imagine how squeamish I felt about it all. So I invited Phil over to the ranch. Phil and I often rode together in the days of our youth although, truthfully, I could ride circles around him.

"We sheepishly shook hands and, mounting our steeds, we galloped off deep into the fields. Or, at least, I did. Philip's horse was a wild one, it seems, one that didn't take well to being spurred. Phil was thrown in a matter of minutes. I rode back to help. My horse spooked. There was nothing I could do. Phil was lying right in front of my horse. My mount reared and reared again, pounding the earth with its front hoofs. Pounding. Pounding. Pounding.''

The President paused for a moment. "Poor Philip. He was trampled to death, I'm afraid. The most decorated soldier in World War II, killed by a reckless animal. I was saddened, of course. But I vowed that, if elected governor, I would continue in the stalwart political tradition established by my best friend. I was elected by a landslide."

Traveler sighed. "What's the point, Frayling?"

Frayling's composure eroded further. "The point, my misguided mercenary, is that if I could eliminate one of the greatest soldiers in history in a few minutes with no struggle whatsoever, just think how quickly and how easily I can plow through you!"

Traveler shrugged and nearly tipped forward. He pulled himself back into his kneeling position. "The mind boggles."

Frayling's voice was sputtering. "Just who do you think you're talking to?" he demanded.

"A squirrel's idea of Utopia," Traveler muttered with a smirk.

Traveler nearly fell face first into the sand as a bony hand ripped the blindfold from his eyes. Unrelenting white light caused him to cringe. He turned his head away from the rays of the sun, then raised it gradually as his eyes refocused. Frayling was standing before him in a battered walker, a Colt .45 in his right hand.

Traveler attempted a smile. He was too tired to complete it and let it fade from his lips as a lopsided frown. He caught a hint of movement to his right. He slowly turned and saw a young Mexican male, about eighteen years old, kneeling in an identical position. His hands were also affixed firmly to his ankles. The kid was wide-eyed and petrified. He glanced at Traveler. The boy couldn't force himself to look at the scarred old man in the walker.

"What did the kid do?" Traveler asked Frayling.

"Nothing," the President replied with a nonchalant shrug. "He is what we call a visual aid. As you can see, he is in the same predicament you are. His arms are aching. His knees are raw. His back is pushed into an unnatural shape. He is afraid that if he falls to the side or backward or forward, he'll be killed."

A twinkle played through Frayling's remaining sighted eye. "He's right, of course. What he doesn't know, though, is that it really doesn't matter what he does. His fate has already been decided.''

Frayling cackled softly and raised the handgun before him, bringing the barrel to a halt a foot in front of the boy's head. The President squeezed the trigger once. Traveler shut his eyes. He heard the boy exhale sharply, both out of surprise and grief. *Whoosh*. Like a balloon whose knot has suddenly come undone. *Whoooooosh*. And then . . . nothing. The sound of something light collapsing on the sand.

The President lowered his hand and the revolver back to his side. "Now"—he smiled at Traveler—"shall we discuss the whereabouts of your friends and that baby one more time?"

19

Hill and Orwell sat motionless in the Meat Wagon. The baby, Alexander, busied himself in his makeshift bed, examining an old army blanket and making appropriately impressed cooing noises when he came across a particularly interesting tear.

The bodies of the horse-creatures were still sprawled, torn and mutilated, in front of the van. A grim reminder of the explosive power hidden beneath the tranquil desert surface.

Orwell sighed. "Well, we sure as hell can't go forward."

Hill nodded. "I'm not so crazy about shifting into reverse either."

Orwell agreed. Maybe the desert behind them was totally clear. Maybe there'd be no problem. Then again, maybe they had been just plain, dumb lucky driving this far. Maybe the path they had traveled was littered with mines and they had simply and miraculously avoided slamming over one.

Orwell glanced out his window. "We could drive off to the left."

"Yeah," Hill said eagerly, "and skirt *around* the minefield."

The hopeful look on Orwell's face faded. "Except that we don't know that the minefield doesn't start directly to our left."

Hill picked up the train of thought. "Yeah. And even if it didn't start there, we don't know how big the minefield in front of us is, how far to the left it stretches. I mean, we could think we were driving around the sucker and then, *kablam*, wind up diddy-bopping right through it."

Orwell sighed. "I guess that goes for the turf on our right too."

"I guess so," Hill said sadly.

The two men stared at the carcasses of the horses in front of them. Buzzards were beginning to feed on the still-steaming innards. The birds were safe as long as they landed on the animals. One or two of the carrion eaters, however, showing caution in approaching the corpses, landed on a vacant patch of desert.

Several explosions rocked the afternoon silence.

The buzzards became part of the al fresco lunch scene, post haste.

Hill and Orwell winced as the mines went off.

"Well." Orwell sighed. "You know what we have to do."

Hill wiped a trickle of sweat off his forehead. "Yeah, and I don't like it."

Orwell shifted his massive black frame behind the wheel and made a move to open the door. "Since I drove us into this mess, it's only fair that I walk point."

Hill rested a restraining hand on Orwell's shoulder. "What, are you kidding me? I was always the best point man. Besides, a guy your size would probably set off every mine within a two-mile radius as soon as he put one of those size twelves outside this van."

Orwell smiled. He grabbed Hill's hand awkwardly. "Hey, if anything happens . . ."

"Nothing's going to happen," Hill said, scurrying to the back of the Meat Wagon. "Let's see what I can throw together back here."

Hill grabbed three yard-long pieces of metal tubing, used for the construction of the odd pipe bomb. Snatching some twine, he tied them together one after another, slightly overlapping, to form a seven-foot-long length of pipe.

"This is about as wide as this tow truck," he muttered, looking at his handiwork. "Now, I need a handle."

Grabbing one of the lightweight assault rifles, he emptied it of its clip and tied it to the metal rod, barrel first. He formed something that looked like a poorly formed T, an object boasting a shortened stem and an elongated crossbar at the top.

Hill kicked open the back of the van and tossed his construction to the ground. He then turned to Orwell, "Well, s'cuse me, Missuh Orwell, I gots to do mah sweepin' now."

Orwell smirked. "Racist."

Hill looked at the child in the cradle. The baby gave him a long, piercing stare. "You take care of this kid, Orwell. If I hit anything out there, promise me you'll make it to the border, warn President Jefferson and . . . take care of the baby."

"Of course I will," Orwell lied, knowing full well that if Hill *did* discover a stray mine, all three of them would be heading to the next astral plane before anyone could take care of anything or anybody.

Hill placed the metal bar in the sand and, crouching over, began pushing on the rifle stock. From a distance he resembled an aged, old cripple pushing a dust broom across a very dirty floor. If this "broom" hit anything solid, however, the floor would erupt like a volcano.

Hill walked forward some three feet.

The metal bar pushed harmlessly through the sand.

Orwell shifted the Meat Wagon into reverse and slowly traced Hill's path.

"Slow down," Hill hissed. "Let me get a good twenty feet ahead of you before you start to follow. With you on my tail, if I set one of these mothers off, the car's going to go up like a skyrocket."

"You don't think I want to sit around here by myself, do you?" Orwell asked.

"You have the baby to think about," Hill said.

"Either way, my friend," Orwell said, continuing to back up. "I don't figure it matters much if I stay three feet behind you or thirty. If you find one mine, I'm bound to find another trying to get out of here."

"I've always hated you when you were logical," Hill muttered, edging the metal rod forward.

The minutes grinded away silently. Sweat poured down Hill's face. His back ached from the effort. His hands stung from gripping the rifle stock so tightly. He felt as if he could hear every grain of sand as it cascaded up and over the metal rod.

"I feel like I should be singin' a song or something," Hill said. "You know, like those movie guys did when they were marching off into war."

"What movie guys?"

Hill pushed the metal bar forward. Three more feet. Five more feet. Ten more feet. No explosion yet. "Oh, I don't know. Remember all those John Wayne films? When he was in the cavalry? They'd ride off to fight Indians singing songs about the flag and stuff."

"Then what would happen?"

"The Indians would usually beat their asses."

"They probably heard them singing a mile away."

"Oh, yeah," Hill said, still shoving the metal bar ahead of him. "I never thought of that. Well, maybe like in *The Man Who Would Be King*. Remember that one? They sang some old Limey song before the natives made them fall off a cliff. Maybe I should sing one of those."

"Whatever you like, my friend," Orwell grunted, guiding the van in reverse. He angled the car carefully. Should the Meat Wagon go outside Hill's seven-foot path, it ran the danger of hitting a stray mine missed by the metal rod.

Hill stood straight for a moment, took a deep breath, and was about to sing a stirring British song when he remembered that he didn't know any. The closest thing to a British anthem he remembered was "The Mighty Quinn" by the Manfred Mann band. And that didn't really count, because that had been written by Bob Dylan. Hill paused. He wondered if Bob Dylan was still alive.

Hill was at a loss. Singing the National Anthem or "America, the Beautiful" seemed too ironic considering the present circumstances. He shook his head, bent back down, prodded the metal rod before him again, and began singing the only long-winded song he could remember.

"A hundred bottles of beer on the wall, a hundred bottles of beer, if one of those bottles should happen to fall, ninety-nine bottles of beer on the wall. Ninety-nine bottles of beer on the wall, ninety-nine . . ."

The sky was torn apart by a resounding blast. Hill froze. He was afraid to look around. He glanced straight down at his feet. They were still there. It hadn't been him that had just been blown up.

"It's okay," Orwell said nervously. "Another buzzard just made a bad landing."

Hill nodded and nudged the metal rod forward again. "Ninety-nine bottles of beer on the wall . . ." he continued.

The metal rod rolled onward. Six feet. Ten feet. Twelve feet. The Meat Wagon slowly trailed behind, still purring in reverse.

"Eighty-one bottles of beer on the wall . . ." Hill allowed his voice to trail off. "How far have we backed up?"

"Maybe twenty feet," Orwell said. "Twenty-five. It's hard to tell."

"Shit," Hill hissed. "I'm gonna be shiftin' sand all god damn day at this rate."

He straightened up and stared at the desert ahead of him. "Awww, fuck it. Sand is sand. A mine is a mine and dead is dead, no matter how fast or how long it takes, right?"

Orwell stared at the man behind the van. "Yeah, I suppose."

"Well, then eat my dust." Hill cackled. He let out a deranged Tarzan yell, grabbed the stock of the rifle barrel, and ran forward, propelling the metal bar through the sand wildly. Sprays of sand shot up as Hill trotted onward.

"Hill!" Orwell yelled. "You crazy son of a bitch. You want to die?"

"If I do go," Hill called behind him, "I don't want to go of old age."

Orwell watched Hill gallop off into the distance. A large grin appeared on his sweating face. "Yeah." He nodded. "I can dig that."

Slamming his foot on the accelerator, Orwell sent the Meat Wagon skidding off after Hill in reverse.

Hill continued running, head bent over the sand. "Screw the sand, screw the mines, screw death, dyin', fightin' and my Aunt Martha, who was the biggest bitch I ever seen in my whole fuggin' life," he roared, plowing onward, half expecting to blow up with every step.

He ran like a madman, his feet plowing into the sand ferociously. Sweat slid over his body in a solid wave. He felt like a snake shedding its old skin.

"Whooooie," he bellowed. "Make way for the express."

After galloping dizzily for a mile, Hill collapsed onto the sand. He rolled over on his back, cackling. The Meat Wagon pulled to a halt at his feet.

Orwell stepped out of the van and hit the sand solidly with his left foot. "No mines."

"Nope. Screw the mines. Screw the sand. Screw . . . Aunt Martha, I'm sorry. You weren't *the* biggest bitch—"

Orwell extended a massive hand down in Hill's direction. Hill grabbed it and allowed himself to be pulled to his feet.

Orwell patted his friend on the back. "Man, you've got balls. If that was me, I would have been pissin' in my pants."

Hill flashed a knowing grin. "I was."

They both looked at the endless expanse of sand before them. "Now," Orwell said, "all we have to do is figure out how to get *around* something we can't see."

Hill nodded. He heard a few stray barks echo in the dunes behind him. Wild dogs. A pack of them, probably. Attracted by the smell of fresh meat. "I think I have an idea," he said.

Orwell grinned. "I'm one step ahead of you." He grunted. He hoped they could rig things up quickly. He had no idea how far away they were from the border but he did know they had just lost an hour's time . . . an hour when that army of Glory Boys and mad monks could be gaining ground.

At that point, the baby began to cry. "Yeah," Orwell said to the child in the van. "I know just how you feel."

20

Traveler didn't mind the fact that he was going to die. That, somehow, had always been a given with him. If he got out of any situation with all his fingers and toes intact, he considered that a substantial plus. In this world, in his profession, death seemed like breaking even.

The wound on his side was in constant pain. It felt like someone had stuck a bayonet through his flesh and now was slowly twisting it. He realized he had a fever. In fact, it was probably the only thing keeping him alive. The fever allowed him to wink in and out of present tense, to abandon reality in favor of fantasy.

His head was pounding. His eyes felt as if they would explode any second. Yet the fever, throwing his body into spasms of harsh yet relieving chills, gave him the freedom to focus his attention somewhere else.

No. Traveler didn't mind dying. He only wished it would happen a little more quickly. He was beginning to get bored with Frayling's concept of torture.

He was only vaguely aware that the withered form of the former President had been replaced by the more porcine figure of the self-appointed pope of madmen, Gordon Peissler.

Peissler was sitting on an old crate, wearing a flowing, blood-red robe. Traveler gazed up at the sweating man. Peissler seemed to be as tall as a skyscraper. Traveler couldn't figure out exactly how the deranged religious leader had grown so. He made a move to scratch his forehead in bewilderment but found that he couldn't move his arm, or his hand, or his legs, or any part of his body for that matter. It was then that he realized he was buried, up to his neck, in sand.

Traveler chuckled to himself.

Quaint.

"What's so funny?" Peissler asked as Traveler slowly slid into consciousness.

"Better be careful what you plant," Traveler rasped. "Ye shall reap what ye sow . . . isn't that from the Bible?"

"Not mine," Peissler said, resting his elbows on his knees and then cradling his double chins in his open palms. "Personally, I think this whole scene is a bit melodramatic, you know? But Frayling wants it played this way and both his Glory Boys and my brethren seem impressed, so what the hell? We'll dig you out in a little while."

"That would be nice."

"Look, Traveler. We have this problem, here. Let's talk about it man to man, okay? Merc to merc. Frayling has a large bug up his butt about you and your friends. That's his business. That's your business. You and I both know that the man has plenty of room in his attic for extra furniture, if you catch my meaning. But he may be back in a position of power someday, so it makes good sense for me to play along.

"I don't want to take on any of your President Jefferson's soldiers. That's not my style."

"Right," Traveler said. "You stick mostly to underdeveloped countries. Kill them with kindness, right?"

"Hey"—Peissler grinned—"I didn't say I was *perfect*. Besides, most of those jerkwater countries have benefited from my invasion. I gave 'em religion, right? Now they have a center in their lives. They have something to orbit. It takes their minds off other worries.

"But, like I said, I have no great desire to take on any government troops. Frayling doesn't either . . . at least not yet. That's why he wants to stop your friends. He thinks they'll bring some stateside opposition down south. Me? I don't care. I'll just turn around and go back to my own kingdom as soon as I see any sign of them. Your friends are no threat to me at all. All I want is that fucking little baby. Now is that so much to ask?"

"Frankly, yes," Traveler said.

Peissler began massaging his furrowed brow with a bloated hand. "I don't understand you at all. What the hell is one kid in this crazy world?"

"Exactly," Traveler agreed. "Why all this fuss for one kid?"

"I can't let this drop," Gordon said with a growl. "You know that. I've backed myself into a corner with this religious mumbo jumbo. That old priest made a prophecy, loud and clear, bellowing at the top of his skinny little lungs. If I don't kill that kid, I'll be in disgrace. Worse yet, I'll lose my grip on these people. They're loyal to the point of suicide . . . but that's only because they believe that God is on my side. If they think that the second messiah is out there, somewhere, ready to lead them to a new, promised land, what the hell do you think will happen to me? At the very least, they'll leave me flat. And what the hell is a leader without anyone to lead?"

"A very reflective person."

"Yeah, well, I've done all the soul-searching I want, thank you. Just tell me where the kid is and I swear I'll get you out of here in one piece."

Traveler stared at Peissler. He knew that Frayling would never allow him to leave the camp alive. In truth, Traveler had no desire to leave the camp alive. His body was half shot. His mind had only a tenuous grasp on reality. And, as long as he kept up the snappy patter and prevented this rag-tag outfit from blundering on, he served a vital purpose. He was a great stall for time. And the more time he wasted, the more time he gained for Hill, Orwell, and the kid.

Traveler smiled at the pope. He didn't mind dying if his death served some purpose. "No sale," he whispered.

"Jesus, but you're dumb," Peissler said, getting to his feet.

A second figure, reed-thin and cadaver-white, hobbled into view. Frayling had returned to gloat. "Any luck, Gordon?"

"No."

"No *what*?"

"No, sir."

Frayling placed both hands on the front bar of his walker and gazed down at Traveler's head. "Well, perhaps the good lieutenant would be more talkative if he was dealing with a more persuasive party."

A tall, thin, cowled figure stepped out of the background and took his place behind Peissler. He whispered something in the pope's ear. Gordon nodded and frowned, shooting the President a disdainful look.

The President pulled his hands off the walker and, balancing his frail body precariously within the metal rack, clapped his hands twice.

Traveler was dimly aware of the sound of hoofbeats. The smiling Frayling maneuvered his walker backward quickly, like a crab avoiding a fisherman. The pope and his angular accomplice backed away as well.

The air around Traveler seemed to tremble. A large black object crashed not six inches in front of his face, sending a spray of sand over his eyes. He attempted to blink it away. He couldn't. His eyes snapped shut involuntarily, scorched and running. He allowed his head to rest on one side. The thunderclaps continued all around him. He was vaguely aware of strange, slender shadows pounding the earth all around him.

Frayling watched with disappointment as three Glory Boys astride their whinnying mounts galloped around and around Traveler's head, missing him by inches.

Frayling noted Traveler's disinterest. "Why doesn't he react? Why doesn't he flinch?"

"The guy's half dead," Peissler said matter-of-factly.

"Damn him," Frayling muttered. "He's always spoiling a good time."

The angular monk whispered again into Gordon's ear. The fat man nodded and turned to Frayling. "What happens if one of the horses step on his head?"

"Sploosh." Frayling wheezed, laughing. "It'll go sploosh. I've been waiting a long time to see that."

"Yeah, well, what if Traveler knows where his buddies are? If his head goes 'sploosh,' then his mouth clams shut, right?"

Frayling stopped laughing. He considered Gordon's words. For a dumb, slovenly mercenary, the man occasionally displayed a good deal of common sense. Frayling was too emotional. He realized that. That was a bad trait. It almost had been his downfall. When he started the last world war, he was in a very bad mood. He had just lost $2,345 in a poker game with his chiefs of staff, his wife was going to be *very* pissed off, and then, to top *everything* off, the Soviets had to start rattling their sabers.

Well, that was the last straw. He was a man who couldn't be pushed around. He had proven that point damned well. Of course, it nearly ruined him, with the nuclear aftermath and all, but he had done pretty well since then, considering the odds.

He watched the horses skitter around Traveler's head. "All right," he called to the Glory Boys, "dig the bastard up."

Gordon looked at the President expectantly.

Frayling was lapsing into his militaristic mode now, a posture he had picked when he had starred in a couple of dozen *B* movie serials. "We'll move out now. We've wasted enough time."

He pointed a bony finger at Traveler. "He's our prisoner now. We'll continue questioning him as we go. Let him linger awhile. Let him think there's hope. The illusion of hope can make men do many things."

Gordon rolled his eyes. Practically that entire speech was lifted from *Hellcats of America*, a 1958 opus featuring Frayling as an intrepid sailor, still wet behind the ears, who winds up commanding a submarine when the officers keel over from food poisoning during the height of World War II.

"I'll have Brother Diablo," Gordon said, nodding toward the tall monk at his side, "take care of the prisoner."

"Diablo, eh?" Frayling said, breaking into a lopsided grin. "I like that name."

Frayling extended a gnarled hand in the direction of the long-limbed, robed figure. "Put it here, Diablo."

The monk did not respond.

"He doesn't understand a word of English," Gordon interrupted. "And, to be honest, what he knows in Spanish doesn't qualify him as a genius either. But he's loyal and true and most important, an expert in torture."

"Really?" Frayling said, pulling his hand back.

Gordon held up one of Brother Diablo's large, dirt-caked hands. "These paws could probably get a rock to cry mama. He's an artist when it comes to pressure points."

"Wonderful," Frayling said, clamping his walker. "I couldn't have wished for a better companion for our lieutenant."

The President glanced over his shoulder. Two Glory Boys were yanking Traveler out of the sand. Each had his hands

wrapped around Traveler's armpits. Traveler's body was limp.
Dead weight. That made the task even more difficult. The Glory
Boys swore under their breath. Frayling couldn't be sure, but he
swore Traveler was laughing.

The President turned to Gordon. "Tell your man to keep
working on our prisoner. Meanwhile, we're going to make a
beeline for the border. I want this attack to be a total surprise. I
just hope that his friends haven't alerted the authorities already."

"Attack?" Gordon blurted.

"Yes, yes, I know it may come as a surprise to you but I've
had it planned for a while. You didn't think I was raising an
army just to *defend* myself, did you? No, no, Gordon. I plan to
regain my rightful position in America. I've been planning a
sneak attack for months. It will make Pearl Harbor look like a
Sunday picnic."

He gestured toward Traveler. "This—this meddling mercenary
has forced me to accelerate my schedule somewhat, but maybe
it's for the best, eh? After all, now I have *you* and *your* men
in the ranks. Still, I'd feel better if I knew where his friends
were. They saw too many Glory Boys down here. If they alert
the authorities up north, the new army will have its guard up."

Pope Gordon was still in an advanced state of shock. "Attack?
Attack? But—but, we're hardly a match—"

"True, true." Frayling nodded, motioning toward his limousine. "But my men have been on the C.B. for the last eighteen
hours gathering our forces together. Some, of course, won't
make it in time. But others—our desert strike forces—have ral-
lied with remarkable speed."

Gordon thought that the President had finally lost it. The old
man had turned and was hobbling toward the awaiting limo.
Gordon was about to comment when Brother Diablo nodded his
head toward a vast sand dune behind them.

Gordon swung his massive frame in the dune's direction. For a
second he thought he was hallucinating. Over the dune marched
Glory Boys. A few thousand of them. Soldiers and their slaves as
far as the eye could see.

Gordon's jaw flapped up and down. He heard Brother Diablo
mutter something in Spanish, ending with the word "loco."

Gordon gazed at the retreating figure of the cackling President.

Frayling was actually going to invade the United States with a hastily formed but massive guerrilla army!

The plan was so simple, it was perfect.

No one would expect it. After all, everyone north of the border assumed that both Frayling and his Glory Boy units were history. Bleached bones in a nuke-out.

But here they were, alive and well and spoiling for a fight.

Gordon didn't know whether to panic or to relax. He was caught in a wave that was gathering momentum. He was a leader being led.

The crippled President slid into his limo. Gordon watched one of Frayling's aides fold the walker and stick it into the backseat. The President continued to cackle.

Gordon watched the man in amazement. He was loco, all right, loco like a fox.

21

Traveler marched behind a jeep, his hands shackled together, his legs wobbly. He could barely focus his eyes. Sand and sweat formed a death mask over his face. He was in a walking fever dream, a delirium.

He was surrounded by Glory Boys. It was the largest, wildest contingent of fighting men he had seen in years. These were hardcore villains: professional soldiers gone bad marching side by side with thieves, murderers, and frightened townspeople who had been kidnapped, browbeaten, and, ultimately, thrust into slavery.

Something in the back of his mind alerted Traveler to the fact that he was probably marching in the first military movement that would lead to the second American Civil War. Two Presidents, one legal, one a renegade, fighting it out over the remains of a once-great nation.

The thought made Traveler sag.

His body slipped toward the desert. A slender but firm hand grabbed him under his right armpit and lifted him up. Traveler twisted his head around painfully and gazed into the forbidding face of Brother Diablo. The man's countenance was long and dour. He had high, accentuated cheekbones and a short, pugged nose. His lips were chapped and seared. His blue eyes were firm but not unfriendly. He wore his red hair cut in a short crew style.

Pope Gordon, astride his sway-backed steed, galloped over

and barked out a few commands in Spanish at the slender monk. The monk nodded. He did not speak.

Gordon smiled at Traveler. "You'll be in Brother Diablo's hands from now on," he said with forced jocularity. "He's very . . . capable."

With that, the pope broke out into peals of laughter and rode off. Traveler was puzzled. He glanced at Brother Diablo's face. This guy was about as Mexican as Traveler was.

Brother Diablo seemed to have sensed Traveler's doubts. He smiled thinly. "Look straight ahead. Do not respond. For the record, I do not speak English. Therefore, I am not speaking to you now and you are not hearing a thing."

Traveler blinked and staggered in the sand.

"Lean on me as much as you can without being obvious," Diablo said. "Your side is a mass of infection. Without treatment, it is only a matter of time before you die."

Traveler stared straight ahead. "Are you my executioner?"

"I am your guard, your torturer, if you will."

"Great. Why are you chatting with your prisoner in a language you don't speak?"

Diablo smiled thinly. "Because I think we can help each other."

"How so?"

"I will help you escape if you will take me to my homeland."

"Where's that?"

"America, of course."

Traveler laughed. The man's English was stiff and stilted, the kind heard on language instruction records. Every syllable seemed like a new word. Every letter was pronounced. "You don't sound like a native."

"I have not been home since I was three years old. My name is Hanratty. Thomas Michael Hanratty."

"Yeah. I didn't think you looked like a Diablo, with that carrot top."

Brother Diablo shrugged. "Brother Diablo is a survivor. He does what he is told to stay alive. He feels no sorrow. He feels no joy. He is an instrument of the pope."

"You're kidding me. You actually work for Peissler?"

"When in Rome . . ."

"But Peissler is a walking lesson in anti-Darwinism!"

Diablo gripped Traveler tightly. "I don't have time for sanctimony. My father was the American ambassador in Bolivia when the nuke-out occurred. I wasn't even a teenager then. He was killed in the riots that followed. I fled to the jungle. I became a guerrilla fighter, a loner.

"When Peissler's religion invaded South America, I made myself useful. I decided it would be better if he never knew my origins. He doesn't trust Americans in his ranks. He's afraid they'll outthink him. So I fell back on my Spanish and became Brother Diablo. This is the first time I've spoken English in nearly fifteen years. Forgive me if it sounds strange."

Traveler stumbled and nearly fell. Diablo held him upright. The robed figure continued to whisper. "I have heard that America is in just hands again. Is this true?"

"As far as I know," Traveler said.

"Then you must warn your leaders of Frayling's plans."

"Invasion?"

"Immediate surprise attack. He has limited small-arms weaponry but a lot of men; men so bored and tired of confinement that they would attack a battleship if they were ordered."

"How far are we from the border?"

"Not too far. I cannot be sure. But Frayling seems to be anxious. That would suggest he is nearing his goal. He has already called in his air support."

"What?" Traveler blurted.

"Yes, another surprise. Since I speak no English, people feel free to jabber in front of me. Last year Frayling began collecting any and all aircraft he could. Not only does he have a few vintage planes plundered from Mexico, but he managed to locate a few private jets and a few dozen somethings called Chingkooks?"

"Chinooks," Traveler muttered. "They're transport and supply copters. Big suckers. They could easily be modified for battle. What about fuel?"

"In South America there were plenty of fuel depots left untouched. After the war the locals panicked and rioted against their local governments and, after a while, even each other. They succeeded in beating themselves senseless, leaving them wide open for any invading army.

"Enter Peissler and his church. They just walked in and took anything that was valuable. Up north, however, Frayling and his

Glory Boys beat him to it. There were a lot of oil refineries standing unattended in Mexico. People were more worried about getting their crops started again than in burning gasoline.''

"So Frayling just rolled in and took over."

"It looks that way. He has plenty of fuel of all sorts."

Traveler's mind began to race. Things were changing now. He couldn't die just yet. He had to find Orwell and Hill. Barring that, he had to make it to the border himself and before Frayling. The deranged President now presented a very big threat to the struggling new democracy in America. Someone had to warn the people up north what was heading in their direction.

And who would the saviors of the New United States be? Maybe two mercenaries and a baby or, perhaps, a dying Traveler and an Irish-American monk named Diablo.

Traveler couldn't help but laugh.

"What's so funny?" Diablo asked.

"Everything," Traveler said, without meaning it. "Do you have any plans for escape?"

The thin figure shook his head. "All I know is we have to act quickly. There's a chance we will reach the border by nightfall. If we do, then everything is over. If we don't, then tonight will be the last chance we will have."

Traveler nodded. Maybe it would also be the last chance America would have.

22

Hill and Orwell sat on their haunches outside the Meat Wagon. In front of them, in the sand, was spread the contents of a few old tins of Spam. They looked at each other nervously. Orwell attempted to appear calm. Hill, however, made no pretense at nonchalance. He was scared out of his wits.

"I sure hope this works," he hissed.

"We've got to give it a try," Orwell emphasized. "It's the only way to get around those mines."

"Yeah," Hill acknowledged, "but wild dogs are not your household, buddy-boy type animals. They don't like people. Hell, they don't even like other wild dogs. They are *nasty* mothers."

"Uh-huh," Orwell nodded.

"I mean, I seen little wild dogs eat real big people."

Orwell sighed, wishing Hill would shut up. "Uh-huh."

"And we're supposed to convince a pack of wild dogs to just let themselves be roped and tied to the front of the Meat Wagon and then lead us through the desert like some Yukon King huskie geeks?"

"No, we don't have to convince them. We have to rope them and tie them to the front of the car. They'll run forward. If we give them enough rope and there's a mine in front of us, the dogs will get it and we won't. They'll be our minesweepers."

"Yeah, well, I know it's the only thing we can do, but those dogs aren't going to like it."

"We don't have to tell them."

Hill looked at the Spam. "Oh. Okay. Hey. How do we know they're going to want to eat Spam and not us?"

"We don't."

Hill nodded thoughtfully. "Oh."

Hill scrambled to his feet and sat on the back of the van. Inside, baby Alexander was staring intently at the roof of the vehicle. Hill looked at the little green-eyed boy with wonder. "Man. I bet there won't be many kids on your block who'll have had this kind of upbringing."

The baby turned his head toward Hill. He didn't smile or make a sound. Somehow he was looking *beyond* Hill. The look caused Hill to shiver involuntarily.

He turned back to Orwell. "I like this kid and all but sometimes he really gives me the—"

Orwell didn't speak. He squatted at the rear of the van, paralyzed, staring out into the desert.

Hill slowly turned his head to see exactly what held Orwell's interest. He wished he hadn't. Twenty of the meanest, most scab-ridden wild dogs he had ever seen stood menacingly not ten feet away. Neither Hill nor Orwell had heard them approach. The dogs hadn't growled. They hadn't barked. They had done nothing to betray their presence.

From the looks of them, they were part shepherd, maybe part wolf. They were two to three feet high and deep-chested. Their snouts were long and angular, their eyes beady. Pointed ears were positioned straight back. They were waiting for something.

Froth dribbled from their mouths.

Much to his dismay, Hill noticed that not one of the dogs was focusing its attention on the Spam.

Orwell made a slight motion with his left hand. He was moving it gradually toward the coiled ropes at his side.

The dogs turned, as one, and glared at his hand. Orwell slowly pulled it back. No. He didn't think he was going to be doing much roping today.

Hill stood, transfixed, at the back of the Meat Wagon. Now what? If the humans made a false move, the dogs would be on them in a second. If the dogs bounded forward, all Hill or Orwell could do would be to shoot as many as they could. Either way, it didn't look like the Meat Wagon would be aided by mine-tripping canines.

Hill finally got enough courage to speak. "What are we going to do?" he croaked.

The dogs tilted their heads inquisitively to one side at the sound of Hill's whine.

"Beats the shit out of me," Orwell said with a sigh.

The dogs regarded the men carefully. Who were these interlopers? What did they want? How would they taste?

Hill was close to tears. After surviving all this time and making it through all those battles, just to meet your doom like a common can of Alpo. It just didn't seem fair.

"Do you think we can rope *any* of them?" Hill babbled.

"You're joking, right?" Orwell shot back. "If I make one move for those lariats, it will be my last."

"Aren't you going to *try*?"

"Nope."

Hill's knees began to shimmy. He was ready to faint. He leaned back against the van with a thump. The dogs turned their heads at the sound and stared intently at Hill. Hill began to sink slowly toward the sand.

The dogs began to advance as a unit. Slowly. Deliberately.

Hill gazed in horror at each drop of saliva oozing out of their mouths onto the sandy desert floor.

The insanity of the situation finally hit him. There was no way he could fight them off. His rifle was inside the car.

All Orwell had strapped to his side was a Colt .45.

Not exactly the strongest of defenses.

The dogs continued their ravenous advance.

"It's not fair!" Hill suddenly shouted.

The beasts stopped momentarily at the sound of the raised voice. They were about to continue their march when the stillness of the desert was ruptured by a high-pitched yowl.

The baby had begun to cry.

The dogs froze in their tracks, confused and apprehensive. Hill and Orwell exchanged quick, hopeful looks. The dogs began to whine softly. There was no doubt about it. Something in the crying moved them.

"Reach in the back of the van and bring the kid out," Orwell hissed.

"I can't do that. Those dogs will turn him into an appetizer."

"Maybe not. Maybe they'll freak out and scatter if they hear the kid at full volume."

"Suppose he stops crying when I pick him up?"

"Then pinch him and start him squealing again. Christ, Hill, will you yank that kid out here?"

Hill cautiously reached a hand inside the van and slowly pulled Alexander to the rear of the vehicle. He lifted him up and, cradling him in his arms, pointed his mouth in the dogs' direction.

The child abruptly stopped wailing.

"Oh, shit," Hill muttered.

He pinched the baby. The baby, gazing intently at the dogs, didn't seem to feel it. He held his tiny hands out in front of him, waving at the dogs in short, spasmodic moves. All the while his eyes were trained on the pack.

Hill pinched him again. "Jesus," he whispered to Orwell, "the kid feels no pain."

Orwell looked first at the baby and then at the pack of wild animals. Something weird was happening.

The baby continued to eyeball the beasts. The dogs stopped whining. They didn't attack. Instead they returned the child's gaze. Finally one dog stepped forward, its tail wagging.

As Hill and Orwell watched, amazed, the very features of the dogs seemed to change. Their eyes suddenly didn't look all that predatory. Their ears were cocked forward, alert but not threatening. A few of them sat down, tails wagging. Others simply walked back and forth casually.

The baby smiled and clapped his tiny hands together.

The lead dog trotted up to Orwell and placed his snout directly in front of the black man's nose. Orwell wondered if this was the vision he would take with him to the grave.

"It was nice knowin' you," Hill muttered.

The dog barked once, nearly sending the petrified Orwell flying backward. He then gave Orwell a Brobdinagian slurp and trotted to the front of the van. He began to bark in a quite cheerful manner.

Orwell sat, wiping his face off. "The thing *licked* me."

"What the hell is going on here?" Hill asked no one in particular.

The baby continued clapping his hands together. The other

dogs began to bark and, following their leader, trotted to the front of the van where they started to prance and yap about.

"Get in the Wagon," Orwell ordered.

Hill didn't reply. He placed the baby inside the Meat Wagon and climbed in behind him. Orwell slid into the driver's seat. The dogs continued to hop around in front of the battered vehicle. Orwell turned on the ignition.

As if on cue, the dogs trotted slowly off, still yapping, before the Meat Wagon. The animals would trot ten or twenty feet and then turn expectantly toward the van.

Orwell followed cautiously. "It's as if they want us to follow them," he said incredulously. "It's as if they *knew* they were supposed to lead us out of here."

"This is screwy," Hill said, still not believing his eyes.

"Maybe so," Orwell said, slowly watching the dogs and tensing his body for the possible detonation of a mine. "But, if you ask me, this is one for the record books. File this one under miracle."

"I don't believe in miracles," Hill said, shooting a suspicious glance at baby Alexander. The boy child was sprawled contentedly in his crib, a blissful smile on his face.

"Miracles ain't natural," Hill said firmly.

Outside the van, the dog pack continued to frolic as they led the vehicle out of danger.

"Ain't natural at all," Hill repeated, still observing the child.

23

"Any sign of them yet?" Andrew Frayling barked from the back of his limousine.

"No, sir," replied a Glory Boy trotting alongside the car on an exhausted horse.

"I don't like it," Frayling muttered to no one in particular. "They couldn't have just disappeared into this desert. We should have at least found their van."

"Sir?" the Glory Boy injected. "May I suggest that perhaps they did just that. Perhaps they died and the desert sands have covered their bodies."

"You may suggest that, soldier, but I wouldn't come near believing it."

The President motioned the young soldier off with a wave of his gnarled hand.

"Stop the car," he commanded. His driver did as he was told. Frayling stuck his head out of the right rear window and gazed behind him. A few thousand soldiers rode and marched through the twilight. The men were growing weary. Frayling realized that. As much as he hated to lose time, if he continued to push his troops to the point of exhaustion, they wouldn't be very effective when it came to launching the attack tomorrow.

Frayling watched the sun disappear behind a parade of fluffy, cumulus clouds. Night would fall momentarily. He decided to allow the men to rest for six hours. They would strike out again shortly before midnight, under the cover of darkness. With any luck, by late morning tomorrow they would be across the border and raising havoc with the Jefferson's border patrol.

Frayling signaled for Pope Gordon to move forward from the ranks. The obese holy man spurred his horse onward. Coming to a halt next to the limousine, Gordon stared down at the skeletal figure in the backseat.

"Yes, Mr. President?"

"Tell the men we will be camping here for a while. They now have a few hours to eat and sleep. We'll march again shortly after midnight."

"Excellent idea." Gordon nodded, uttering a sigh of relief. Another few miles and his god damn horse would have dropped dead.

The word was spread by riders charging down the lines of marching men.

Traveler and Brother Diablo, now located toward the rear of the parade, nodded perfunctorily as the messenger trotted by.

"Luck is on our side," Brother Diablo said, pushing Traveler into a sitting position in the sand.

"That's a change of pace." Traveler moaned, hitting the sand harder than he had expected to.

The tall, redheaded man in the flowing robe settled, crosslegged, into a spot across from his prisoner. "Will you be strong enough to flee?"

Traveler was numb from his neck down. He shook his head affirmatively. "I'm very resourceful."

"Good," Diablo said. "I have been thinking of a possible means of escape. While the bulk of the troops sleep, both Gordon and Frayling will undoubtedly send out men, probably in pairs, to scout ahead."

"Point men."

Brother Diablo gave Traveler a quizzical look. Traveler explained, "The forward man in a combat mission. The guy who takes the flack if the enemy is setting a trap."

"Ah, yes." Diablo nodded. "Well, there will be a point team tonight, no doubt. We have to be part of that team. Once we get far enough away from the troops, we just keep on moving."

"Sounds good to me but just how are we going to be appointed to the pep squad?"

"It will be dark. It shouldn't be too difficult to wander off, providing we look the part."

Traveler stared at his battered body. His combat boots were scuffed. His pants were torn and bloody. His vest was mangled. "I don't think I'll pass for anything but a prisoner."

"I'll get a robe for you. Tonight you'll join Pope Gordon's flock."

"Hallelujah. Religion at last."

Diablo motioned for Traveler to be silent. At that point Gordon Peissler waddled over to the two men, his crimson robe dotted with sweat stains.

"Enjoying the scenery, Road Ghost?" He grinned at Traveler.

"Uh-huh," Traveler wheezed. "It's the accommodations that could be improved."

Gordon lifted a heavy shoe and was about to smash it into Traveler's head when Brother Diablo intervened, placing a brotherly arm around the rotund mercenary-turned-demigod. "He hasn't talked yet. We must keep him conscious," Diablo whispered in Spanish. It was a simple but sensible statement.

Peissler frowned and grunted. He would have loved to draw blood but he saw the wisdom in Diablo's words. "Well, keep working on him," he replied in Spanish in a conspiratorial tone. "Let me know if he starts talking. Let *me* know, not Frayling."

"As you wish, your Holiness," Diablo said, executing a reverential bow.

The lanky redhead watched Peissler march away. Traveler hadn't understood the exchange. He tried to read some meaning into Diablo's expression. Diablo didn't *hate* Gordon. He clearly didn't care enough about him to hate him, or even dislike him. He was just an obstacle, a hurdle to be cleared. Tonight Diablo was planning to do just that.

"I'm going to shackle your legs now," Diablo murmured, producing a chain from beneath his cowl. "I'll send another monk over to guard you while I go up front and check to see what their plans are. Try not to antagonize the guard. He just might kill you. Gordon's followers are an impetuous lot."

The lean man chained Traveler's ankles firmly together and, after motioning to a young, bearded monk, strode off toward the front line.

Traveler didn't say a word.

His new guard was short, barrel-chested, and smelled like a barnyard. The bearded monk glared at the prisoner. Traveler wondered if this was one of the monks that Peissler had gelded to prevent little Alexander from being born.

Traveler turned his eyes away from the monk and stared at the gathering darkness above. It seemed like eons since he had thought of the tiny boy child and his friends. He wondered if they were all right. He wondered if they had made it across the border.

A shooting star appeared from nowhere and plummeted toward the earth.

24

The pack of wild dogs zigzagged through the sand, their coats glistening in the moonlight. Trailing behind them cautiously, the Meat Wagon rumbled through the barren wilderness. Orwell gripped the wheel, a look of astonishment on his face.

"Look at those pups go!" he muttered. "They're not even winded."

Hill sat behind him, gazing out the windshield over the driver's shoulder. "They're not pups. They're wild dogs. They're killers, crazed animals. And we're following them like lentils—"

"Lemmings."

"We're still following them like *they* know what they're doing and we're some dumb boots just out of training camp."

Orwell carefully guided the van in the path that the dogs had cleared in the sand. "Damn straight we're following them. They haven't hit one land mine yet, have they?"

"No, but—"

"No buts, Hill. I don't know how they're doing it or why they're doing it, but those dogs seem to know just what part of this desert is safe and what part has death written all over it. As long as they don't go boom, this boy is following."

Hill glanced behind him. Baby Alexander was fast asleep. "I still think it's spooky, man," Hill said. "Did you see how those mutts reacted to the kid here?"

"Children and animals are simpatico," Orwell theorized.

"Not *that* simpatico. There was something going on out there, Orwell. Something not natural."

"Miracles happen."

"No way. We're talking something real but something screwed up."

Hill looked at the sleeping baby. "You don't think this kid is a mutant of some kind, do you?"

"What are you talking about?" Orwell frowned. "He's a beautiful baby. He's perfect. He's handsome, well behaved, he knows when to cry and he knows when to snap to."

"Maybe he knows *too* much."

"Maybe you talk too much."

"I'm serious, Orwell. He's only two days old. He's an infant, for chrissakes. He takes his formula with no sweat. He doesn't fuss about like other babies. And when he looks at you, he *looks* at you. He doesn't just stare at you, gaga-eyed. He looks at you like he recognizes you, like he understands every freakin' word you say."

"What are you, a pediatrician?"

"All I'm sayin' is that maybe I don't know a lot about little kids, but I do know that this little kid don't act little."

Orwell focused his attention on the dogs. He wouldn't admit it aloud but even *he* felt that the baby's behavior was a little too perfect. Still, there had to be a logical explanation for it.

"Look," Orwell offered. "For all we know, baby Alexander may be in shock . . . or he may have suffered brain damage. Neither one of us is a doctor. We deliver a premature child after the mother is murdered, butchered. And what happens after the baby is born? He gets taken on a joyride in the back of a van through a desert.

"He runs a fever, gets a massive dose of antibiotics, and is fed formula that is at least twenty years old. What you perceive, what *we* perceive, as his quiet intensity may just be that the kid is punchy.

"For all we know, he's on the baby equivalent of a trip, a hallucinogenic experience. God knows he's been subject to enough body- and mind-stretching encounters since he's been born. Maybe his nervous system has just shut down or something to protect him.

"Of all people, *we* should understand that. Remember what we were like after the neurotoxin scrambled our senses? We'd be sitting somewhere almost catatonic, comatose to the world at large, while inside our bodies and brains were writhing."

Hill rubbed a calloused hand over his stubble-strewn jaw. He felt vaguely guilty now. "Yeah. You may be onto something there."

"I'm not saying that you're wrong and I'm right," Orwell concluded. "All I'm suggesting is that there are a lot of possible reasons for Alexander behaving like he does. For all we know, we could be the cause of it."

The van hit a bump. Orwell was tossed up in the air high enough for his head to slap hard against the ceiling of the Wagon. Hill slammed into the side. His right shoulder hit the bulletproofed wall with a resounding thud.

"Shit," he hissed. He turned to check on the baby. Alexander was awake now, staring dully at Hill. Hill stifled an involuntary shudder and bent over the child.

"You okay, kid?"

The baby flashed Hill the warmest, most gleeful smile ever seen on a child's face. Alexander extended his tiny hands forward and clapped them over and over again. Hill laughed and tweaked the child's nose with his right thumb and forefinger.

"Yeah, you should laugh. Your uncle here has been acting like a real dope. When you get old enough you'll learn what battle fatigue is like . . . or if you're really lucky, you'll never have to worry about it at all. Maybe some day people will stop—"

The van swerved wildly to the left.

Hill heard Orwell swear under his breath.

"What's going on?" Hill asked.

"Damned if I know," Orwell replied, grappling with the wheel. "The dogs just started zigzagging."

"Why don't we just pull away and take off? Kiel is going to have one hell of a time finding us if we don't make it to the border soon."

Orwell heaved a colossal sigh. "Hill. We might as well get it through our heads that it is very likely Kiel is dead."

Hill twisted his body around to face Orwell. "No way. He's gotten out of bigger jams than—"

"Hill, he was half dead when we left him."

"Hey! The guy is a professional soldier. All he had to do was get his hands on a jeep or a horse and—"

"The odds back there were about five hundred to one. I don't like to think that we'll never see him again."

Hill didn't respond. Orwell was greeted by total silence. He stirred in his seat uneasily, adding, "I love that man like family. We're brothers. But we have to start considering the fact that he might be dead."

Hill pounded his fist into the dashboard of the Wagon. "Bullshit! Bullshit! We all made it through El Hiagura. We made it through the fuckin' nuke-out. We have to stick together. We have to. We can't just . . ."

Orwell lowered his voice. He couldn't yell at Hill. All the man was doing was voicing the very feelings Orwell had rumbling around in the back of his head. "Hill," he said softly. "There were four of us in El Hiagura: Paxton, Hill, Orwell, Margolin. Margolin's gone. Then there were three. All I'm saying is that we should be prepared for the three becoming two. I'm not saying that it has happened. I'm not saying that it will. Kiel might be a couple of miles behind us right now. Then again, he might not. I'm just saying we should think about the fact. That's all. Just think about it and act accordingly."

"Yeah, well," Hill muttered, "that sucks."

Orwell sighed. "Yeah. It sucks."

The dogs veered wildly again. Orwell wrenched the wheel, sending the Wagon into a fishtail. Sand sprayed up over the windshield.

"Where the hell are we going?" Hill demanded.

"I'm just driving," Orwell explained. "I figure these dogs have been right so far, so why tempt fate?"

"Let's split from the dogs and head north," Hill said. "Kiel— even if Kiel is—we *still* have to get across the border and tell Jefferson about the number of Glory Boys living commando style down here."

"I know that," Orwell replied, watching the dogs dart to and fro before the van. "But what happens if the dogs are leading us through another minefield right now? If they are and I veer off, we become one with the cosmos."

"In other words, those dogs are calling the shots."

"It looks that way."

"That *really* sucks."

Orwell nodded. He couldn't argue logic.

"Are we at least still heading north?" Hill asked.

"I don't know," Orwell replied. "Lean forward and check the compass."

Hill stuck his torso between the driver's seat and the weapons rack in the front of the van. Affixed to the dashboard was an old, reliable compass. At least, it was reliable once. Now its needle was spinning round and round, like a wheel of fortune at a two-bit carnival.

Hill pulled his body back into the rear of the van. "I should have figured," he mumbled.

"What does the compass say?" Orwell asked.

"The compass isn't working," Hill replied. He squatted down and stared through the windshield at the sky above. "It's a clear night. Maybe we can figure out what direction we're heading from the stars."

"I didn't know you were into astronomy," Orwell said.

"I'm not. I thought maybe you could figure . . ."

"Nope," Orwell said, spinning the wheel and allowing the van to slide across a sand dune, hot on the dogs' trail. "I never was a boy scout."

"Damn," Hill said, still gazing upward. "I think I see the Big Dipper. Does that mean anything?"

"It means we keep on following the dogs."

Hill sat down in the Meat Wagon and folded his arms angrily. "Man, I hate being out of control."

He turned and looked at baby Alexander. "I hope you're taking notes, kid. This is the weirdest trip I've ever taken in my whole adult life, and you're getting it as a special introductory offer."

The baby clapped his hands and giggled.

Hill settled down in the back of the van. "Yeah. Maybe you've got the right idea. Maybe we should just sit back and enjoy the ride."

The pack of wild dogs sliced through the swirling desert sands under the watchful gaze of the moon.

The battered van shadowed their every move, its driver muttering a deeply felt litany of curses.

25

Brother Diablo stood in the moonlight, a faint breeze rippling through his cassock. He had pulled the cowl from his head and now his face, illuminated only by the night sky, seemed to be the personification of death. Dark circles clung to the skin beneath his eyes. His cheeks were sunken, his mouth recessed. It was less a face than a mask, the mummified remains of something that was once lively and vital. It was a frightening sight for Traveler to behold.

It was even more frightening for the bearded monk guarding the battered mercenary. Diablo motioned for the guard to bring Traveler out of the crowd of dozing soldiers. The bearded man nodded dumbly and yanked Traveler to his feet by the chains wrapped around his wrists. Since Traveler's legs were shackled as well, the most he could do was hop after the monk. Pain tore through his ruptured hip with each movement.

Diablo turned on his heels and marched off into the night. The puzzled guard followed, dragging Traveler off by the wrists. When Diablo had walked a few hundred yards away from the main encampment, he stopped and faced the guard.

The monk stood at attention. Diablo motioned for the bearded man to let Traveler go. The guard took the order literally and simply released the prisoner from his grip. Traveler went tumbling onto the sand. His head snapped backward with a thump, sending his already reeling senses spiraling further toward total stupor.

He managed to roll over on his side. He watched, awestruck, as Diablo approached the monk. The tall, redheaded man passed by the guard as if dancing a ballet. He waved his hands slowly through the air in a gentle, fluttering motion as he slid by the other monk. Diablo turned and faced the guard. Without explanation, the man collapsed onto the desert floor. His neck had been broken. Traveler blinked, half believing he was hallucinating. He had never even seen Diablo touch his victim.

In one graceful move Diablo pulled the robe off the dead man and tucked it under his arm. He bent over Traveler and grasped the chains around his wrists. Sliding his hands to and fro, he broke the chains in two.

Diablo caught the puzzled look on Traveler's face. "There is nothing mysterious about it." He smiled thinly. "I will teach you all there is to know once we reach home. America."

He yanked the chains off Traveler's ankles and handed him the robe. "Put this on. We will walk up to the front of the camp on its left flank. They are sending out the forward guards now. We will simply walk past Gordon and your President—"

"He's not my—"

"—and join the guards leaving camp."

Traveler slipped into the robe. It wasn't a bad fit, considering. He pulled the cowl over his head in such a way that his face would be obscured even on close inspection. Diablo pulled his hood up over his head and set off toward the front of the encampment with a deliberate stride. Traveler, shorter by nearly six inches, had to double-time it to even keep up. He nearly stumbled twice. Walking in a robe was not the easiest thing in the world to pick up in a few seconds.

He saw Diablo slacken his pace. Traveler did the same. A group of Glory Boys and monks were being armed and sent out in different directions. Most were on foot. Some were on horseback.

Traveler didn't like the looks of the setup. In order to pick up the heavy assault rifles being issued, both he and Diablo would have to pass dangerously close to the bloated figure of Pope Gordon. Gordon might not recognize Traveler as a monk but he was bound to spot Diablo.

Traveler glanced at his companion. If Diablo was worried, he showed no signs of it. Traveler sighed as Diablo got in the line leading to the weaponry. Trust an Irishman to tough it out no matter what.

The weapons were stacked in the back of a jeep. The line of would-be point men was moving slowly but smoothly. Everything seemed to be working. Gordon wasn't really paying attention to who was in line and who wasn't. Traveler kept his head lowered inside the hood. He did his best to look humble as he shuffled by the pope.

All was going well until the line abruptly stopped moving.

Gordon looked up. "What's the problem?"

"Ran outta rifles," the driver of the jeep announced.

"Well, go back to one of the six-bys in back and pick up some more. We want this area combed tonight."

The driver slipped behind the wheel of the vehicle and drove off, leaving a dozen or so monks and Glory Boys in line. Gordon glanced casually at the waiting point men. His face was passive, almost bored, until his gaze focused on Diablo. The tall, wiry monk was doing his best to look neither tall nor wiry. Gordon, however, was sending his cognitive powers into overdrive. His eyes were squinty now. He was either forming a massive thought or a large pocket of gas.

"Brother Diablo?" Gordon said, rushing toward the line. "What are you doing here? Where is your prisoner?"

The fat charlatan stopped in his tracks, eyeing the short monk behind Diablo. "You!" he said, pointing an accusing paw at Traveler. "What are you . . . *guards!*"

Diablo shrugged and flipped the cowl from his face. He reached under his robe and tossed a battered Fairbairn-Sykes fighting knife to Traveler. Traveler tore open his robe and caught the knife as he leapt out of the religious gear. He tossed the knife from hand to hand. It was good to hold a weapon again. The knife was a straight-bladed, double-edged cut- and-thrust weapon. He squeezed his fingers around its oval handle and gauged its weight. Three quarters of a pound. Eleven and a quarter inches in overall length.

"*Guards!*" Gordon was still bellowing.

Diablo and Traveler found themselves surrounded by a mass of club- and knife-wielding monks. Diablo had no trouble out-maneuvering them. He twisted and turned his body, grabbing arms and breaking them. A bald Glory Boy, knife drawn, dove at the redheaded assassin. Diablo merely smirked and sent his hand flying toward the man's face, palm outstretched. His palm caught the man's nose and shoved it upward. The cartilage snapped inside the attacker's snout and fragmented, shooting wads of bone up into the Glory Boy's brain. He was dead before he hit the ground.

Traveler spun his body wildly at the charging men. His head was swimming. His vision was blurred. He slashed to his right, turning his palm slightly up and snapping the knife out with an abrupt motion of his shoulder, biceps, and wrist. As the knife dragged through clothes and flesh, he tightened the grip on the weapon, yanking it back to the guard position, poised at his throbbing waist.

Blood was floating in the air everywhere. He blinked his eyes, trying to clear his fuzzy sense of sight. It seemed that the attackers just kept coming. He began thrusting out, aiming his knife at bright white throats, stomachs, groins. He pivoted on his right leg, snapping his blade forward while pulling his left foot, leg, hand, arm, and shoulder backward. He could feel the blade penetrate. He could hear the screams. He didn't know who he was hitting or where.

He glanced over at Diablo. The angular man was choreographing a danse macabre, a dance of death. He kicked his feet lightly in the air, pulverizing hearts, stomachs, kidneys, and groins. He reached out and shattered forearms and wrists of knife-wielding Glory Boys.

Traveler shook his feverish head and, for a split second, the scene became clear. There were three dozen men, dead and dying, all around them. More were on the way. It seemed, for a moment, as if Diablo and Traveler would actually be able to fight their way clear of the point men and flee into the desert.

For one split second Traveler actually felt a sense of hope. He shot a glance at Diablo. Their eyes met. Diablo managed a small smile. He understood that escape was at hand. A roar destroyed the scene. Brother Diablo's head exploded into a dozen pieces. The tall man's body turned and did a graceful circle. His long, slender hands reached up toward his ruptured neck. They seemed to be trying to catch the pieces of skull before they hit the ground. Blood erupted high into the night sky, a crimson foun-

tain defying gravity. The black robe was soon soaked through.
The cadaver crumpled in a heap on the desert.

Traveler stopped midslash. He spun around and faced the
twisted visage of President Andrew Frayling. The President was
gripping his walker. A burly Glory Boy was at his side, holding a
still-smoking shotgun.

The President offered Traveler a lopsided smile. "I hate a fair
fight," he explained.

Something smashed into the base of Traveler's skull.

He pitched forward, body surfing on a tidal wave of agonizing
pain.

In his mind he and Thomas Michael Hanratty shook hands and
stepped over the border into their homeland. America.

26

He was on his back. There was caked blood on his neck. He was spread-eagled on the desert floor. His arms were pulled up and out, ropes fastened around his wrists.

A silent Pope Gordon and a perturbed President Frayling were standing above him.

"I'm having a hard time deciding what to do with you, Lieutenant," Frayling said. "I mean, I'm going to kill you. That's a given. It's the how that's perplexing."

Pope Gordon turned and left the scene. Frayling shook his head sadly. "He's angry. He has every right to be. You and your friends have allowed that child to escape. There's still a chance we'll run into your buddies as we push forward but, if we don't, Gordo's ass is grass. Well, there's no use crying over that now, eh? We have other matters to attend to."

The President dragged his walker around to Traveler's right side. "In a few minutes I am going to launch an all-out sneak attack on America, Lieutenant. The beginning of the end for your new President. I'm going to hit them with everything: by land and from the air. It will be very spectacular."

The old man pursed his lips thoughtfully. "Of course, you won't be able to see that. I'm leaving you behind. The big question running through my mind is this: Should I leave you here in two big pieces or many little ones?"

The President sighed and dragged his walker around Traveler's feet. "It's a very difficult decision for me. The two-piece death

151

would be more spectacular, certainly more dramatic but, alas, also quicker.''

Frayling smiled paternally at the spread-eagled prisoner. ''Ah, but you have no idea what I'm talking about, do you? Well, you will note that your two hands are tied to something very solid above your head. You are firmly affixed to the back of a jeep.

''I did a movie once called *The Barbarian and the Lady*. A good film but not a great one. We filmed it in Spain. The food was terrible. Many of us had the runs. But I digress. There was a wonderful chariot sequence in that movie where the barbarians, of whom I was a leader, would take Christians and strap them to the back of chariots, much in the same way that you are strapped to the back of that jeep. On a given signal, the barbarian chariot drivers would whip their horses and drive their chariots round and around the Colosseum, dragging the Christians around after them. This was considered the big entertainment of the time, sort of an early version of *The Wide World of Sports*. The sport, of course, was watching the Christians slowly have their skin flayed off their bodies. By the end of the afternoon, they all resembled hamburger. Oh, by the way, I stopped being a barbarian by the end of the movie.''

The President leaned back in his walker. ''*That* is method number one.''

Traveler remained silent.

The President ran his tongue along his lower lip. ''Now, method number two comes from another sword-and-sandal epic I starred in, *Whipmaster of Rome*. I played a gladiator who would rather use a bullwhip than a sword. Between you and me, there were no bullwhips back then but the part was so well written, I didn't want to rock the boat. The *New York Times* caught on, though, and gave the movie a pretty good roasting, believe-you-me.''

The President shook his head sadly. ''I still miss the *Times* after all these years. I don't miss New York, mind you. I'm glad that it's gone. A citadel of sin it was, although the view from the Empire State Building was pretty impressive.''

Traveler's head was throbbing. He thought his guts were going to crawl out of his hip wound. His arms ached. His wrists burned from the ropes wound tightly around them. Every fiber of his body was aflame.

"In *that* movie," Frayling continued, "we took a Christian and tied him to two chariots. His arms were tied to the back of one, his feet to the back of another. On a given signal, both chariots took off in opposite directions. Within seconds we had two short Christians where we once had one long one."

Frayling leaned forward. "So, what'll it be: two pieces or lots of little ones?"

Traveler ignored the President. Once, many years ago, when his body's nervous system had first been shattered by neurotoxins, he had practiced a calming mental practice that bordered on the supernatural. He hadn't had to use it in a few years, since the effects of the toxin had gradually worn off, but now was definitely the time to try it out again.

He shut his eyes and sent his consciousness streaming into his body. He located the sources of pain. The stretched muscles. The torn flesh. The twisted limbs. He pushed the pain out of the outermost areas and mentally forced it back to its source point. He then went about mentally isolating the injured areas from each other. He shut down. He compartmentalized. He froze the pain. He reduced it. He lulled it back into slumber.

As his mind instinctively raced through his body, his consciousness drifted. He was no longer in the desert. He was in a green field in a strange land. People were dressed in togas. Perhaps this was merely an echo of the movies Frayling had been talking about. But, no, he had been here before. Perhaps in a dream? Perhaps in another lifetime.

Unicorns frolicked in fields of wildflowers. Children skipped around a maypole. A lean, peaceful man walked up to Traveler and shook his hand warmly. Traveler strained to identify the green-eyed stranger. It didn't matter. He was a friend. Traveler knew that and relaxed. The pains in his body subsided.

Traveler opened his eyes. Frayling was still babbling incoherently. Traveler took a deep breath. The night air smelled fresh and clean. He no longer felt tired. He no longer felt alone. His body, although it still ached somewhat, was no longer a wreck. Traveler felt as if he had been sleeping for days. He was rested and ready to meet whatever treatment Frayling was about to dish out.

"Fine," the President said. "It will be little pieces."

He glanced behind Traveler. "Carl. Start the jeep. You will lead our charge with our friend here bringing up the rear."

Traveler gritted his teeth as he heard the jeep in front of him rev its engine. The President produced a revolver from beneath the folds of his moth-eaten suit coat. He aimed the barrel at Traveler's groin. "And here's a little variation I thought up all by myself . . . just to get things off to a good start."

Traveler refused to turn away. The President smiled, released the safety on the gun, and pulled the hammer back.

"The Lord works in mysterious ways." Frayling cackled. "Just think, Lieutenant. You thought you were put on this Earth to be a hero. In truth, you were put on this earth to be squashed by me."

A flying ball of fur appeared out of the left corner of Traveler's line of vision and tumbled through the air between Traveler and the deranged old man. The President screamed in pain. When the ball had finished passing by, Frayling no longer held a gun in his outstretched hand. In fact, he no longer had a hand to extend. Blood spurted from the old man's wrist.

Traveler swiveled his head wildly to the right. The air was echoing with cries of alarm. There, not two feet away from Traveler's face, still holding the President's severed hand (and gun) in its mouth, was a large gray wild dog.

The creature leaned forward, dropped the hand next to Traveler's head, and wagged its tail.

As Traveler stared at the beast, he noticed that the noise in the background had changed. The cries of alarmed humans now gave way to the growls of angry beasts.

Traveler tipped his head back and watched, dumbfounded as a pack of frothing dogs descended on the campsite from the darkness of the desert.

27

Traveler didn't know whether to laugh or cry. He tried to shake some comprehension into his mental faculties. President Andrew Frayling was stumbling backward in his walker, screeching, a demented crustacean in an ill-fitting suit. His hand was lying in the sand a few feet away from Traveler's head.

Pope Gordon had erupted into a full-tilt retreat, his legs pumping furiously, his sand-spattered robe flapping in the breeze. Glory Boys and monks were in various stages of flight. Dogs were leaping over Traveler's spread-eagled form. A shotgun blast tore through the air behind Traveler. A fine spray of blood sparkled as it cascaded down around him. Traveler surmised that the driver of the jeep had just been customized.

The roar of an angry engine buzz-sawed somewhere nearby.

Traveler had no idea what was happening behind him, although he didn't mind having the chance to ruminate on the possibilities. It beat the hell out of being dragged across the desert from the rear of a speeding jeep.

A bayonet cut through the ropes affixing his wrists to the auto.

"Jesus Christ! I knew you hadn't bought the farm," came a familiar voice.

Traveler began to laugh. "Hill?"

Hill reached down and pulled Traveler to his feet. "Who else?"

Traveler turned around and saw Orwell behind the wheel of the Meat Wagon. Orwell flashed him a thumbs-up sign. Wild dogs were yelping and diving everywhere. Traveler was still confused. "How did you manage to find me?"

"Damned if I know," Hill said, prodding Traveler toward the Meat Wagon. "I think little Alexander had something to do with it."

"But he's just a baby," Traveler said.

"I have a feeling he's not *just* anything," Hill said. "Let's split before your fan club decides to—"

Small-arms fire sizzled over their heads. "Too late," Hill concluded.

Hill and Traveler dove into the back of the van as Orwell slammed down on the accelerator. The Meat Wagon's back wheels sent up a fine spray of sand as the van fishtailed back into the desert.

The wild dogs, hearing the van's roar, turned their attention from the screaming men and scampered off after the vehicle. Before long they were flanking it.

Traveler, sitting dazed in the back of the Wagon, watched the dogs, astounded. "Where did you pick up the tailed troops?"

"They volunteered," Hill said.

Bullets zipped by the retreating van as the dogs charged ahead, taking the lead. "Here we go again." Hill sighed.

The dogs turned abruptly toward the left. Orwell swung the Wagon in the same direction.

"Is it my imagination or are we following a pack of wild dogs?" Traveler muttered.

"It's a long story," Orwell called over his shoulder. "Trust us."

Traveler leaned back against the bulletproofed side of the van with a sigh. Baby Alexander gurgled at his feet. "Well, at least you're all okay," Traveler said. "How's the kid here?"

"The antibiotics checked the fever. Can't say I understand it. But you know how kids are," Hill muttered, clambering toward the slots at the back of the van. "Full of surprises."

Hill peered out one of the gun slots at the rear. "Jeez. We're in for it now."

Traveler snatched a heavy assault rifle and crawled to an

adjacent slot. Behind the van raced a line of pursuing monks and Glory Boys that stretched a mile. Trucks, jeeps, horsemen, and foot soldiers trailed after the Meat Wagon. They were fanning out in an attempt to outflank the retreating van.

"Where the hell did *they* all come from?" Hill gasped. "There are thousands of them!"

"It's Frayling," Traveler said. "He's planning to invade the states."

"Frayling?" Hill replied, confused. "I thought he'd been deep-fried up north!"

"Only partially," Traveler replied. "We've got to beat him to the border. He has a ramshackle air force strung together as well. He's going to hit Jefferson on two fronts."

The dogs veered to the left. Orwell followed. "Damn," Orwell said. "I wish I knew where we were heading."

"You mean you *don't*?" Traveler exclaimed.

"Nope," Orwell said matter-of-factly. "Where they go, I follow."

Traveler placed the palm of his right hand on his forehead. "Am I still feverish?"

"Those aren't *ordinary* dogs," Orwell began.

A burst of machine-gun fire slammed into the back of the van. Six jeeps carrying Glory Boys appeared from behind a sand dune and began tailing the Wagon not three hundred feet from its rear.

"They're firing low," Traveler said, sticking the barrel of his rifle through the slot before him. "They're trying for the tires."

Traveler squeezed off a burst at the pursuing jeeps. Orwell swung the Wagon wildly, first to the left and then to the right.

"Orwell!" Traveler bellowed. "How the hell can we draw a bead on these guys if you keep driving like a maniac?"

"I'm following the dogs," Orwell called.

"Oh," Traveler said sarcastically, "as long as you're following the dogs, that's okay, then."

The Glory Boys behind the Wagon opened up in earnest. Bullets slammed into the tear-shaped vehicle as Orwell continued his zigzag path. The Meat Wagon sailed over a sand dune, sending Traveler and Hill tumbling backward toward the driver's seat.

Traveler attempted to right himself. His hip slammed into the weapons rack. He winced in pain and fell to his knees. Looking toward the back of the van, he caught sight of baby Alexander. The green-eyed kid was staring intently in Traveler's direction, a small, calm smile on his tiny lips. For no reason whatsoever, Traveler suddenly felt at ease.

He allowed the rifle to slip from his grasp and, turning, focused his attention outside the windshield at the wildly leaping dogs. "This makes no sense whatsoever," he muttered.

"You should have seen us twelve hours ago," Orwell mumbled, fighting to keep the van on course. "In comparison, *this* is an exercise in total logic."

Hill fought his way back to the rear slots. "They're gaining on us."

"Of course they're gaining on us," Traveler explained. "They're traveling in a straight line while we're snaking through the desert like a—"

A series of explosions rocked the Meat Wagon. Orwell laughed out loud. "God bless you, bow-wows!"

Baby Alexander giggled and clapped his hands. Hill let out a war whoop.

Traveler tumbled to the back of the van. He pulled himself up to one of the two gunslots and peered outside. The ground behind the Meat Wagon was erupting into fiery life. Two of the jeeps were in the process of disappearing in a large ball of fire.

The remaining vehicles were tumbling through space in slow motion, their passengers flailing and clawing at thin air as the desert floor rose up to meet them in bright orange belches.

"Minefield?" Traveler asked.

"Yup," Hill replied. "The dogs have a knack when it comes to runnin' through 'em."

"Amazing," Traveler marveled.

"That ain't the half of it," Hill acknowledged.

Traveler watched as the rest of Frayling's army charged onto the massive field of explosives.

He held his breath as the scene unfolded. He had never experienced anything as surreal in his life. The calm expanse of desert behind the van slowly rumbled into action. The earth itself began to undulate and explode, spiraling upward in brilliant

plumes of red, yellow, blue, and orange. Men who had been
standing upright suddenly split in two and sailed this way and
that.

Horses seemed to evaporate in large, purple clouds of fire-
tinged smoke.

Jeeps and trucks shattered before launching themselves heavenward as their gas tanks ignited.

Debris of all kinds, metallic and fleshy, catapulted through the
air. It twisted and turned and then, hitting the ground, set off
other charges and leapt back into the heavens again.

Traveler placed his rifle on the floor of the fishtailing vehicle
and picked up a pair of spyglasses. He peered through the
binoculars beyond the curtain of smoke.

He caught sight of President Andrew Frayling, his bleeding
wrist wrapped in a tourniquet, leaning against his battered limousine. Pope Gordon was at his side. Peissler was pointing a
cherubic hand in the direction of the Meat Wagon. He was
probably bawling about the new messiah getting away, Traveler
reasoned.

Frayling barked something at Peissler, who ignored him. The
President produced a revolver from inside the limo and leveled it
at the rotund man in the robes. Peissler fell silent.

The President wore a determined, deranged look on his face.
He produced a small C.B. mike from the back of the car and
began yelling into it. Traveler didn't like that at all. He would
have preferred Frayling to simply charge through the minefield
and transform himself into half a pound of ground round.

Frayling's and Peissler's men fell back. As the smoke cleared,
Traveler watched the fractured army turn and withdraw, allowing
the Meat Wagon safe passage.

"We did it." Orwell beamed, still following the canine brigade.

Hill tumbled up to the front of the van, emitting a series of war
whoops. "Let's hear it for the canine corps!" He laughed.

Traveler remained silent.

The sun had already fallen below the horizon when the dogs in
front of the Meat Wagon slowed down. Orwell did likewise. The
leader of the pack halted. His companions did the same. Orwell
pulled up alongside the dogs.

"What do you think it means?" Hill asked.

"Maybe we're out of the minefield," Orwell ventured.

Traveler hopped out of the Meat Wagon. "There's only one way to find out."

He walked up to the front of the van, half expecting to be blown sky-high any moment. The pack of dogs seemed to regard his nervousness with some sense of amusement, wagging their tails and exchanging mirthful yip-yip-yips.

The lead dog approached Traveler warily. The great gray beast sniffed the air in front of him and, after carefully taking stock of Traveler's odor, trotted up to the mercenary and sat at his feet.

"Looks like your job is done, eh?" Traveler said softly.

The dog barked three times, then stood and returned to its mates.

"Yeah." Traveler nodded. "See you around."

The lead dog howled and bounded off. The pack followed suit. Soon the Meat Wagon sat alone in the middle of the desert. Traveler glanced nervously over his shoulder as he climbed back into the van.

"Let's double-time it for the border," he said gruffly.

"What's the rush?" Hill said, watching the dogs disappear into the distance. "We've put plenty of distance between us and those Glory Boys back there."

"Double-time it," Traveler repeated.

Orwell shot Traveler a quizzical look. Traveler was staring behind the van uneasily. "You don't think Frayling is just going to let us get away, do you?"

"He doesn't have much choice," Hill reasoned. "There's a minefield between him 'n' us. Besides, he doesn't want the baby. That fat pope does."

"No," Traveler admitted. "He doesn't give a good god damn whether Alexander is a god, a devil, or a citizen of Atlantis, but he does want our hides for two reasons. One: He hates our guts; two: If we tell Jefferson that Frayling is alive, his surprise attack won't be a surprise."

Hill thought that over for a moment. "Oh," he said. "But, still, how could Frayling possibly . . ."

A sudden dust storm obliterated the desert in front of the Meat Wagon. A floodlight shone across the windshield. Hot lead pellets rained from the dark, evening sky.

"Hit it!" Traveler bellowed.

Orwell sent the Meat Wagon hurtling forward.

"I was afraid of this," Traveler muttered, grabbing his heavy assault rifle and running toward the back of the van.

Hill said nothing as he took his place beside Traveler. The two men stared at the sky above the van. The heavens seemed to be filled with helicopters.

28

Frayling's air force was not all that ramshackle after all. Maybe he had salvaged a few World War II bombers. Maybe he had scraped up a few transport choppers, Chinooks. But the sleek, angry helicopters buzzing the Meat Wagon like vengeful wasps were a lot more formidable than anything Brother Diablo had described back in the Glory Boy camp.

They were Spookys: gunship helicopters with miniguns mounted under the nose and at the doors. A minigun could spit out 6,000 rounds of ammunition per minute.

As the bullets sent up plumes of sand all around the twirling van, Traveler didn't see anything cute about either the choppers or their nickname.

The Meat Wagon slogged on valiantly.

"We're not going to be able to take this much longer," Orwell barked after a minute or so. "It's raining lead out there. *Literally*."

Traveler cursed to himself, trying to angle the barrel of his heavy assault rifle upward enough to catch the belly of one of the flying beasts. He squeezed off round after round. The choppers seemed invulnerable.

The Meat Wagon pitched forward to the right. "They got one of our tires," Orwell bellowed.

Traveler crawled to the weapons rack next to the driver's seat. "Anything out there suitable for cover?"

"Negative," Orwell replied, straining his eyes to see past the hurricane winds of dust buffeting the van. The Spookys were firing so hard and so fast that the van's hood was peeling away under the force of the pockmarks. In another minute or so the bullets would rip the engine to shreds.

The Meat Wagon slumped backward.

"Another tire," Traveler commented, peering through the shattered windshield. "Look!" he suddenly exclaimed. "Up ahead. Rocks."

Orwell peered through the haze and the headlight glare and saw what Traveler was talking about. Half a dozen small boulders, each about six feet high, were tossed together in the middle of the desert. It wouldn't provide much cover but it would be a lot better than sitting in a moving metal coffin. The boulders would also afford them a better chance to fight back. The men would be able to fire at the choppers from any angle, without having to worry about gun slots or roofs or a suspension system that had just about had it.

Yeah, the boulders would do just fine.

The trick would be to get there in one piece.

The Meat Wagon shuddered and collapsed in the sand. "There go the other two tires," Traveler shouted to Hill. "Grab two rifles and as many clips as you can. We're going to make a run for it."

The choppers continued to rain down a sizzling torrent. Bullets whined everywhere. The copters' rotary blades continued to produce a tornado of sand and grit. Traveler slung his rifle over his shoulder and grabbed baby Alexander. He clutched the child to his chest. "I hope you realize this is all your fault," he whispered.

The baby whimpered as Traveler hugged him close. "Well, maybe not *all*," Traveler amended, "but a lot."

Traveler kicked the back of the van open. Hill, Orwell, and Traveler dove out into the maelstrom of bullets, sand, and searchlights. For a moment all three were blinded. Traveler spun around in nearly a full circle, squinting.

"There!" he pointed.

The boulders stood not sixty feet away.

Traveler led the charge, Orwell and Hill on either side. firing their guns at the swooping choppers. Bullets sang. Engines roared. Floodlights blinded the men as they ran desperately onward.

Traveler heard Orwell yell "son of a bitch."

A loud *ka-thump* nearly knocked his legs out from under him.

He wondered if the Glory Boys were lobbing grenades now. He didn't have time to ponder the thought. The boulders were dead ahead. Traveler scrambled up and over the first rock, landing on his knees within the sole crevice he could find. Hill tumbled down after him, still firing his gun wildly.

Hill squeezed off round after round, cursing and crying at the swooping choppers. Traveler placed Alexander next to the largest of the boulders and grabbed his rifle.

"Where's Orwell?" he asked.

"There," Hill said, pointing, "the stupid nigger bastard."

Orwell was sprawled, face down, not ten feet from the boulders. The choppers fixed his body within their floodlights and continued strafing his back.

"God damn slow bastard!" Hill yelled. "God damn big flat-footed, size-twelve, asshole bastard! Why did you have to go and do that for?"

Hill fired at the choppers. "Leave him alone! Leave him alone!"

Hill was coming unglued. Traveler realized that and somehow didn't mind. Something inside him was unraveling as well. To come all this way for nothing. . . .

Hill sat down with a thud against Traveler. "Shit," he said. He turned and faced Traveler. "This is another nice mess you've gotten us into."

Traveler nodded and flashed Hill a slightly deranged grin. "Well, what the hell. . . ."

As if on cue, both men stood in the boulders, fully exposing their position to the choppers. Grasping the rifles to their midsections, they fired burst after burst. One of the Spookys caught the barrage head on. Bullets smashed through the cockpit, slicing the pilot into what would pass for dog food. The helicopter began to waver. It hesitated in the air before beginning to spin madly through the sky. As it swung around, it clipped the main rotor of a second aircraft.

Both of the choppers went down like marionettes suddenly robbed of their strings. They hit the desert floor with a resounding thud. There was a heartbeat of silence before they erupted in a fireball that resembled Vesuvius during its finest hour.

"Whooooo-eeeee," Hill yelled. "Two for the price of one."

The remaining choppers raked the boulders with round after

round. Something in the back of Traveler's mind pointed out that, with six choppers remaining, each firing 6,000 rounds per, he and Hill were the targets of 18,000 bullets per minute. He wasn't all that flattered.

The two men continued to pump lead in the copters' direction. Walls of sand cascaded across the rocks. Floodlights shimmered across the desert before skittering up, across, and over the boulders.

Hill continued to yell his war cries. Abruptly they stopped. He leaned back against Traveler. "Well, I'll be damned," he said, sliding down into the crevice. Traveler turned to gape at his companion. Hill was holding his midsection with his free hand. Blood was spurting out from behind his fingers.

Before Traveler could react, the boulders around him began to fragment. The air began to sizzle. A dozen bullets sprayed across his back. More shocked than hurt, he tumbled into the crevice as well.

The two men sat across from each other, mouths agape.

"Holy shit," Hill muttered. "We've bought the farm this time, pal."

Traveler glanced down at his own midsection. His entire front was red with blood. He suddenly thought how it was funny that real blood wasn't the bright red stuff that you saw in the movies but an almost rust-colored, muddy hue. Dust to dust. Dirt to dirt.

Traveler faced Hill. "God damn," he muttered. "I never got my crossbow back."

Hill began coughing in spasms. "What the hell . . . are . . . you . . ."

"They took my crossbow when they took me prisoner. I left without it."

Traveler began to laugh. The things people thought about last.

Hill laughed as well. "You . . . know what I keep on thinkin' 'bout?"

Blood began to dribble out of his mouth. "Remember at the end of that ol' Eddie Robinson movie . . . *Little Caesar*? 'Memember his last words? The guy . . . the guy gets shot . . . machine-gunned, and he turns to the camera and says . . . 'Mother of Mercy, is this the end of Rico?' Heh-heh-heh-heh. That's it. 'Is this the end of Rico?' His name was Rico, ya see. Enrico. He was Italian . . ."

"Hill?"

"Yeah, Kiel?"

"Shut up."

Hill flashed Traveler a ghostly smile. "Sure, Kiel. Anything you say. . . ."

Hill remained smiling and staring. His hand, however, slowly slid down from his chest, exposing a hole as big as a football.

The choppers continued to buzz and strafe the boulders. Lead and rock fragments ricocheted off the rocks, sending small wisps of sand spiraling into the air. Traveler glanced at baby Alexander. No sense in the kid getting fragged. He crawled over to the child and lowered his body over him.

"Well, kid," Traveler whispered, "it doesn't look like you'll reach your first birthday. I'm sorry. I tried. I really tried."

Traveler began to lapse into unconsciousness. The roar of the helicopters drowned out his thoughts. He was suddenly snapped back into reality by a pressure on his forehead. He opened his eyes and gazed directly into the green orbs of Alexander. The baby's tiny hand was pressing on Traveler's head. The baby was staring right through him. For a moment Traveler felt a wave of misplaced nostalgia. He remembered the land where the unicorns roamed and the citizens strolled placidly between pristine pieces of Greek architecture.

A voice echoed through his mind. "Remember."

Traveler tried to retain his grip on reality as the baby pushed him away, backing him against the rock wall. Not knowing if he was actually witnessing the impossible or taking part in a dying dream, Traveler watched as baby Alexander, not a week old, slowly but surely climbed to his feet.

The child strolled confidently over to Hill and placed a hand on his forehead. Withdrawing it, the child scampered up the rock wall. Hill fluttered his eyes. He stared, first at Traveler and then, astounded, at the baby.

Bullets singing all around him, floodlights arcing back and forth, the infant tilted his tiny head up at the helicopters. A strange look played over the baby's face. His features twisted into a misshapen gargoyle's visage. His lips curled. His eyes glowed. His nostrils flared like those of a wild animal.

Traveler shuddered. Was this a god released, a devil unshackled, the birth of a new mutant strain, or a full-tilt hallucination? Whatever it was, it was unearthly and very, very frightening. The child filled his tiny lungs with air and, extending his hands, let out a howl mournful enough to raise the dead. The wind itself seemed to retreat as the child unleashed his power. The baby's cry carried its shrill message upward. Lightning filled the night skies.

The earth shook. The rocks quivered. Traveler tried to pull himself to his feet, succeeding only in teetering up onto his knees.

The helicopters above the rocks abruptly stopped firing. Traveler clearly saw the faces of the men inside, although that was logically impossible, considering his rock-strewn vantage point. Yet somehow he *saw*. Somehow he *knew* what was transpiring. The men aboard the aircraft screamed in horror as their bodies glowed an eerie yellow before bursting into flame. Traveler watched, spellbound, as the men leapt, screeching, from the Spookys, their twisting forms transformed into human torches.

The helicopters hung there, suspended by some supernatural force, until finally, one by one, they, too, erupted into tidal waves of fire and smoke.

The air shook with a volley of deafening explosions.

Hill covered his face with his hands, unable to stand the heat. Traveler felt the violent surge of warmth singe his eyebrows. Yet he couldn't bring himself to turn away from the spectacle. He heard the sound of twisting metal as the choppers plummeted earthward.

Outside the rocks, the landscape was transformed into a veritable hell on Earth. Flames were everywhere. Brilliant tornadoes of red and yellow twisted and turned as they belched up from the wreckage, clambering toward the moon.

Baby Alexander stood unmoved and seemingly unaffected by it all. The child had not budged an inch from his vantage point on the boulder. When the explosions had quieted down to a steady roar, baby Alexander turned and looked, one last time, at Traveler. He offered the mercenary a sly smile.

Traveler shuddered involuntarily. "Remember," his mind commanded.

The baby scampered down from the rock and out of Traveler's line of vision. Traveler crawled up from the crevice. He gazed out from the safety of the boulders into the inferno in the desert. Orwell was propped up, dazed, against the rock wall below

Traveler's hands. Traveler's senses sagged under the weight of the phantasmagoric nightmare awaiting his perusal.

Flames flickered everywhere, hot tongues protruding from the ruptured desert floor. Hot winds blew. Sand filled Traveler's lungs as he peered into the pandemonium.

Baby Alexander stood, triumphant, amid the fire and brimstone. A thick black smoke clung to the ground. From out of the mist, a terrible shadow formed. It moved toward the baby. Traveler tried to shout a warning but found that he was too weak, too disoriented.

The shadow moved out of the cloud of smoke and debris. Traveler found himself chuckling.

"Hoi, hoi, it's the half-breed boy. Gone and found hisself a power that can bring sorrow or joy."

Rat Du Bois nudged his buffalo up to where the infant stood and extended a scarred hand down to the child. The child gazed up at Rat's leathery face sympathetically. Rat nodded and lifted the boy up onto the buffalo. The child had no problem grasping the bison's back, grabbing the beast's hair, and straddling the spine with his tiny legs. He had the reflexes of a miniature athlete.

"Sorry I'm late for my big date with destiny, but the trouble with me is I get carried away with the things I say and before I even know it time has frittered away."

The baby chuckled as Rat dug into the flanks of his beast of burden and angled the bison back into the inferno. Traveler watched the trio disappear into the smoke and ashes, the scarred rider chattering away as the baby laughed out loud.

"It's into the future for you, man child. When people cop to your existence things are going to go wild. But don't worry about that. You're protected by Rat. And there's no one in existence who can track this cat."

Traveler listened to Du Bois's voice fade away behind the staccato noises of the hell on earth.

Then he passed out.

"Remember," the wind said.

29

Traveler awoke in a hospital bed. A male nurse was adjusting an IV bottle in his arm.

The room was painted a piss green. Traveler guessed he was in a military hospital somewhere. Only the government managed to concoct the most unappealing color schemes in existence to aid the wounded in convalescence.

"Where am I?" Traveler said.

"Ah, you're awake," the orderly replied, smiling. "Good. The President wants to see you, *all* of you."

"All?"

Traveler twisted his head to the right. Hill and Orwell were sprawled in hospital beds nearby. They didn't seem the worse for wear. They, too, were stumbling back into reality . . . such that it was.

"But how . . . where?"

"A border patrol found you in the desert not far from here," the orderly replied. "We saw the smoke, couldn't miss it. You three really raised a ruckus out there. Pretty amazing, you taking on those Glory Boys like that."

"Yeah," Traveler said, watching the orderly head for the door. "Amazing. But where . . ."

"Yuma, Arizona," the orderly said before leaving.

"Yuma?" Traveler repeated out loud. "We were heading for California."

"Are you in one piece?" Hill inquired, coming to.

"Pretty much," Traveler replied.

Orwell shook his head slowly from side to side. "Man, I feel like I've been out drinking Black Russians all night."

"Ever notice how biased he is?" Hill replied.

Traveler pulled the sheet away from his chest. He wasn't bandaged. There were no bullet holes. He ran a hand across his face. The only ill effects he seemed to be suffering from were the results of sunburn and exposure. He glanced at his two companions. They were busily feeling about for bullet wounds as well, coming to the same mind-bending conclusions.

"Did we imagine all that?" Hill asked.

"I hope so," Orwell replied. "I wouldn't even want to consider remembering it if there was the slightest chance it was real."

Traveler propped himself up on his elbows, almost dislodging the IV. "Gentlemen," he began, "I think we just made history. I'm not sure how or why but . . ."

"Hey, come on, Kiel, that couldn't been real. I mean, just watch, when that guy comes back in, ask him if he found a kid's body. Little Alexander is probably still lyin' out there, all bullet-ridden and stuff . . . I bet."

"Hill," Traveler asked, "do you remember being hit?"

"Well, yeah. I mean, I *thought* I was hit. I think I thought I was hit."

"Do you remember dying?"

"Nah. Not me. I remember fallin' asleep 'cause I was holdin' my guts in and I got tired."

Hill suddenly glanced down at his unblemished chest.

"Your guts seem to be inside pretty tightly now," Traveler finished.

"Well, *I* remember being shot and I remember dying," Orwell stated. "And *that* scares the shit out of me."

"Jeez," Hill muttered. "I knew that kid was fuckin' weird. Do you know I never even hadda change his diapers once?"

Orwell ignored Hill and turned to Traveler. "What do we do, Kiel? How much do we tell?"

Traveler frowned. "I don't know. We'll tell them about Frayling and Gordon, of course. Have them alert the border patrols. But as for Alexander and Rat and the dogs . . . I think it's best we keep that to ourselves."

"Yeah," Hill muttered. "Where were those guys when I was buckin' for a Section Eight before the big nuke-out? I don't want to be sent to a laughing academy at this late date."

"How will we explain the helicopters?" Orwell asked.

"Maybe we won't have to," Traveler said. "Maybe they've already explained everything away themselves. People in government always have explanations on tap."

"Yeah," Orwell agreed.

The men lapsed into silence for a moment. "You know what really freaks me out?" Hill asked no one in particular. "The fact that baby Alexander is roaming around out there with that freak. I mean, this kid has *power*, you know? I mean, what's he going to do with it? How far will he take it? *What* is he?"

Traveler was about to answer when a middle-aged man in an army lieutenant's uniform came in.

"Gentlemen." He smiled. "Everyone is talking about your great victory. Lieutenant Karl Patton, at your service. President Jefferson is on his way over right now. He's been dying to congratulate you. He'd also like details about the entire affair."

"Of course." Traveler nodded.

"Yeah, no problem," Hill injected.

"As a military man," the lieutenant continued, "I am really proud of your performance out there. Armed only with heavy assault rifles, you managed to wipe out an entire squadron of choppers armed to the teeth—we towed your car in, by the way—armed to the teeth and each filled with a complete crew. Unbelievable. Simply unbelievable."

"I'll say . . ." Hill muttered.

The lieutenant flashed Traveler a knowing grin. "But I've heard all about you and your friends, Traveler. You specialize in making the impossible possible, right?"

Traveler nodded. "So I'm told."

"Tell me," the lieutenant ventured, "just how did you manage to pull that off, anyway?"

Traveler shrugged and slouched back in his hospital bed. "Well, to be honest, it's not hard to overcome any odds. . . ." He smiled thinly "When God is on your side."

Orwell's eyes nearly burst from his head.

Hill launched into a coughing fit.

The lieutenant gave Traveler a snappy salute. "You make me proud to be an American," he said before leaving.

Traveler smirked and leaned back into his pillow.

He gazed meaningfully at the ceiling above.

He wondered how much the body work on the Meat Wagon was going to cost.

And if he could sucker the government into paying for it.